Secrets Exposed

Lisa T. Horton

Washington, DC

Dedication

To God
Thank you for giving me
the strength and endurance.

To my husband
My best friend, we have come so far.
Thank you for your support in everything I do.
I LOVE YOU MORE

To my JHortons
Everything I do is for you

To my friends at the V,
thank you for your support

To Diana
Thank you for seeing my vision
and for all of your teachings.
I'm glad God connected us. I'm forever grateful.

CONTENTS

Prologue

Detective Tommy Little looked up from the charred ground as dawn broke, the sun warming the top of his shiny bald head. The still smoldering house was a total wasteland, and as he walked around the outside, he dug his phone out of his pocket and dialed Vesta Bambino, the county coroner, asking her to come to the crime scene in case they had a body. Besides, he enjoyed having her around.

Detective Shannon Short's suicide a month ago in front of several witnesses had left Tommy with a higher position and some real headaches. Shannon's paperwork was in shambles, and he could not find anything on the last week of her activities with the serial killer case—nothing on her computer and nothing in the messy piles on her desk. Not surprising, as she had been dealing with a lot—a pregnancy from that womanizer named Phillips, and a strange, convoluted situation she had been trying to unravel. It had become personal for her. She had lost it and taken too much responsibility for the case into her own hands.

"We've got a body back here," one of the firefighters said.

Tommy hurried past the crew pounding in stakes and running their yellow tape around the scene, and as he circled the house a bevy of squad cars pulled up. When he reached the part of the structure that had burnt last, he found a couple of walls still intact. A bedroom stood exposed to the morning light, its roof missing and drenched in water. The stench burned his mucous membranes. He should've worn a mask.

Several officers and a firefighter were bent over the body, grimacing. Several others with cameras milled around, snapping pictures. The young woman lay face up on the floor, unclothed, scraps of burnt paper and ashes covering her wet skin, and a half-burnt letter "A" lay just below her breasts. She had a charred place on one thigh and on her torso where apparently a burning board had fallen on her. One ankle was tied to the footboard. An officer bent and placed a couple of fingers on her carotid artery.

"Uh, hey! Got a heartbeat here!" He jumped up and several others sprang into action. Vesta approached and stood at Tommy's side.

"Hi. You got here quick," he said. "You better get up there and have a look at the body before they rush her off to the hospital."

"She's alive?"

"Yeah. Nobody realized it for a while."

Vesta made her way through soggy remains of the small house, the wet mess soaking her work boots. Tommy followed behind, watching her hips sway. He used to watch his ex that way, but no more. She was dead to him. He could almost feel his blood pressure rise from that thought alone, so he focused back on Vesta to get himself out of the disturbing memories.

Vesta spoke to the firefighter examining the victim for broken bones. "Is she conscious? Stable?"

"Unconscious. Heartbeat steady. Can't tell anything beyond that yet. You the coroner?"

Vesta nodded.

"Better get to looking her over before they take her away. She might not survive."

"Thanks, chile," Vesta said, her natural warmth coming out at this tragic moment. She bent down and looked at the young woman's once-pretty face, now scratched and bruised.

Tommy walked around behind the cluster of people who had rapidly gathered, and he tripped on a piece of burnt furniture, taking a moment to get back up. Hopefully Vesta would be done soon so they could leave. Breathing these smoldering remains surely wasn't healthy. When Vesta stood, she was holding a small object between her fingertips.

Inching closer, he asked, "What is it?"

"A pill. Recognize it?"

He moved in until he could look down over her shoulder. His muscles tensed.

"Nope." He scratched the stubble he hadn't had time to shave. He dug in his pocket for an evidence bag. Vesta had done the same.

"Here," he said. "I'll take it."

"I got it," Vesta said.

"No, let me take it. You have your notebook to carry."

She looked at him dubiously. "I think I can handle a little plastic bag and my small notebook, Detective."

"Please, let me carry it for the lady," he said. "I will save her the trouble of getting it to the right authorities." He batted his eyelashes twice.

Smiling at his attempt to be gallant, she handed him the bag.

Bravo, he thought, giving himself an invisible pat on the back.

They watched as the woman was wheeled away, the ambulance screaming off in the still morning air.

Detective Tommy Little turned to Vesta, and with a jerk of his head toward the cars, he said, "Coffee?"

"Only if it comes with a big cinnamon roll," she said. "I think we can afford one this morning."

Her eyes were so cute when she smiled. He let his mind wander a little into "what if" territory as they walked side-by-side to the street, leaving her at her vehicle. "I'll meet you there," he said.

When they were settled at a cozy round table for two with their double-shot lattés and a huge cinnamon roll to share, they discussed the morning's event.

"I have to tell you, Tommy. The woman had abrasions on her throat. Pressure points caused by strangulation. This was attempted murder."

"Oh god, not another one. Maybe it wasn't him, but maybe it was. If only I had more of the info Shannon uncovered just before her suicide."

"It really surprises me that Shannon wouldn't have done a better job documenting her work as she went along." She took her first bite of the hot, gooey cinnamon roll and said, "You know, this isn't the best part of town. Apparently, the woman's name is Briana. She married a year ago and is related to Christopher and Skylar Phillips. She's Christopher's niece. His mother Bobbie lives around the corner in the cul-de-sac."

"And how do you know all these details already, Ms. Bambino? May I ask?"

"You aren't the only one with detective skills, Mr. Little. I am friends with Skylar Phillips and have learned a lot about her and her family. Briana is Christopher's niece. Just married a year ago. Not a nice girl, from what I understand."

"Keep your ears open, and maybe we'll be able to put some of these pieces together eventually, Ms. Bambino." He winked as they got up to leave. She smiled.

Chapter 1

The package, wrapped in brown paper, lay on the mat outside the condo door. Skylar Phillips bent and picked it up. *Ryan Middleton,* the hand-delivered package said.

Skylar rubbed the back of her neck and stretched her sore muscles in the still darkness of early morning. She set the package down in the kitchen, wondering who it was from, then she prepared herself a cup of chai tea and made her way back upstairs with only a nightlight illuminating the stairs. When she reached the second floor, she opened the sliding door to the enclosed balcony, her slipper catching on the lip of the doorframe. She recovered without nose planting on the floor. She was the biggest klutz she knew. Ryan frequently remarked that her clumsiness was endearing, though she couldn't see how. She gazed out at the oceanfront view of the island, tiny lights dotting the edge of the water, and drank her tea. A glow could be seen on the horizon. Most mornings she came out to watch it rise over the clear blue sea as the changing light caused the water to sparkle and glow. She loved this view, especially because she could see how near the condo was to the restaurants and nightlife.

Only a couple weeks left of her three-month Caribbean vacation. How should she spend it? Back in bed with Ryan sounded pretty good. She couldn't have asked for a better distraction to ease the ache of the events she'd tried to outrun. Christopher, that snake-in-the-grass husband of hers who had slept with who-knows-how-many women, deserved to wallow in his losses. She wanted to wallow in Ryan right now, the man of her dreams with the smooth chocolate skin, shoulder-length dreadlocks, and neatly trimmed goatee. Though a bit free-spirited and wild, he knew how to love a woman—unlike Christopher, she thought bitterly.

She took the package with her as she tiptoed back to the dark bedroom, setting it on top of the low dresser opposite the foot of the bed. Though she was still mad that they'd missed the play last week because Ryan was late again, he was her guilty pleasure, so she forgave him. She dropped her short pink satin robe on the floor and slid between the sheets, easing her naked backside up against his warm body. His scented smell aroused her, and she wiggled closer, hoping he'd sense her need. He stirred, then slid his hand over to cup her bare bottom. She remained silent but moved suggestively against his hand. Ryan took that as permission to proceed, and he aligned his body with hers, nuzzling his face in her hair. He kissed the nape of her neck, gentle and slow, his warm breath making her shiver, then he turned her, brushing his lips against hers. The kissing became urgent. A wave of pure pleasure ran through her body all the way to her toes. Her head sank back against the pillow. The first moan escaped Ryan's lips as he found his way, followed immediately by her own, their bodies pretzeled in the most delicious fashion.

"Oooh, baby," Ryan said.

Skylar's cell phone vibrated on the nightstand like a drill.

"Fuck! Are you kidding me? Who the hell is calling you at five thirty in the morning?" Ryan's irritation broke the warm spell.

It had been a couple of weeks since they'd had their feud, but they were horny as wild animals in heat and ready to sex each other's brains out. Nothing else seemed to matter now.

"It could be important." Skylar glanced at the clock.

Ryan whispered in her ear. "Don't answer, baby...please. If it's important, they'll leave a message."

Skylar needed this as much as he did. His manhood was rock hard, so she ignored the phone and focused on her man as he moved with her. When they reached the point of no return, Ryan grabbed her hands and kissed her deeply, their bodies experiencing the usual mind-blowing release they always had together. They lay back in the afterglow, but Skylar couldn't let herself enjoy it long since she had work this morning.

When she finally looked at her phone it was seven o'clock, and the call had been from Christopher. Skylar had just enough time to hop into the shower. She put on her clothes and then sat down at the vanity table to apply her makeup. Ryan's image appeared in the vanity mirror.

"I was up earlier and found a package addressed to you outside the door," she said.

Ryan stared at her with a strange look in his brown eyes.

"What?" she asked.

"You are so beautiful, Skylar. I would have never imagined you being with a man like me. I love having you around. I know you're not going back to Christopher now after what he did. Let's take our relationship further, one step at a time. I love you, baby. I'd love you right." His eyes teared visibly, but he continued. "I'd like to have you move in with me. Even though you feel like my woman, I would have no expectations, however much I might want to."

Skylar paused. He was speaking from his heart. "That's sweet of you, Ryan. I'd like that, but as you know, I have a lot of things to resolve before I can decide what I want for the rest of my life. But I care for you very much."

"I know you can't give me an answer, but I would really like to travel through life with you." He smiled warmly. "Have a good day, baby."

She picked up her bag and keys. "You too. I'll be thinking about what you said. You can tell me about your package when I get home." She swung her bag cheerfully, then moved closer for a goodbye kiss and he gave it, looking at her with affection as he patted her butt. She smiled and walked out, glad he had not asked who the caller had been. She headed down the road toward the store in her jeweled sandals. The department store was close, only a few blocks away, and she always walked. She patted her pocket for her keys, the reassuring jingle easing her mind. She reached the department store and changed into her work shoes just in time to clock in.

Chapter 2

Skylar's temporary job at the local department store gave her enough spending money to be happy, and she had enjoyed the change of pace where she could socialize with a lot of people. One of the things she'd learned about herself through her counseling was how much she enjoyed hearing about the private lives of others, and she had a natural ability to put their life stories into a big picture and help them see where they could improve both themselves and their situations. She didn't mind putting a hiatus on her counseling for now, and she had big ideas about changing that up a bit and doing some relationship coaching, but she wasn't quite ready, especially when her own marriage was such a mess.

Ryan, eager to get back to the mainland, had already begun shipping artwork back. He'd warmed her heart with his invitation. He'd be so easy to live with. She'd already visited his condo and seen his extensive collection of art. She timed in, then walked out on the floor to start her shift. Where'd Ryan get all his money, anyway? He seemed to have an unlimited amount of it. From buying and selling art? Why had she never wondered before? Truth be told, her anxiety had skyrocketed now that their return was near. She'd be starting over, and that prospect did not excite her. Life on the island was laid back and peaceful, and she did not feel rushed to make any decisions.

One of the biggest problems was what to do about her marriage. Maybe the reason Christopher had called was because he wanted to push along on a divorce. Tears sprang to her eyes, but she pushed them back where they came from and pulled her anger back over it, covering the hurt like a blanket.

She moved out onto the sales floor, helping customers and returning the high-end clothing to the racks and shelves. The rest of the day flew by. When she went back to the break room to get her things from her locker, Jason and Julia were there, apparently waiting for her. They greeted her and asked her opinion about their relationship problems. This would delay her from going home, because she couldn't resist doling out advice on people's love lives. And Jason had found a way to thank her that she rather enjoyed.

After Julia left, Jason said, "I got these just for you, Ms. Skylar." He handed her two green tubes with a single joint in each. She smiled and slipped them in her purse. He was young and cute.

"You know I like telling people how to solve their problems, Jason," she said.

He nodded. "You are so good at that. You can zero right in on the problem and know how to solve it. I hope your idea to start your own business will work out. Good advice is worth a lot of money," he said. "We are so glad you came to work here."

"Thanks, you are sweet. You and Julia will be fine, Jason. You're already doing most of the things we've talked about. In regard to my business, I have ideas for a name and a logo, but first

I'll have to go back home. I have things to attend to there before I get this up and running. But I liked your idea to use a butterfly on my logo. That's just the image I want."

Her life had changed so much. As she walked the three blocks back to the condo, she realized she didn't need Nyquil anymore now that she had something better to calm her anxiety. Jason had been a godsend. She'd make his gift last as long as possible.

When she got home, she saw that Ryan had been busy filling boxes to mail back. She would move in with him for now, but eventually she'd get her own place. Sometimes she needed space from others, and she knew she'd want a place she could decorate herself. Hopefully Ryan would understand.

She hugged him and said, "Hey, babe, I came home without my phone. I'm sure I left it in the break room at work."

"You sure it's not in your bag?"

"Yes, I'm positive. That jeweled case is hard to miss."

Ryan snickered at that, as he had teased her unmercifully for her jeweled existence. Her phone, her sandals, her sunglasses, even her purse—all had jewels. She had no clue why she always picked those over others. She barely had any real diamonds that she could call her best friends.

"How was your day?" Skylar asked.

"Productive. Just after you left, I took off to the dollar store to pick up some packaging tape and I've been working on this packing ever since."

Skylar shook her head, still thinking about her phone and wondering why she was so careless with her things in a bonkers world. "I'm not going back tonight. Hope no one steals it. I'll call and ask someone to put it in the safe."

Ryan sat down on the settee and motioned her over. She relaxed into him. "Maybe you'll enjoy the peace of not having your phone intruding into what you're doing whenever it feels like it." He fondled her as he said it. She sighed and encouraged him by squirming into just the right position.

The next day she went early to pick up her phone at work. She had seven missed calls. Two from Christopher and five from Madison. She walked back home, glad of the exercise. When she'd nearly reached her front door, it rang again. Madison.

"Skylar! How have you been? What's been going on? How come you didn't answer?"

"Hey girl, life treating you well?" Skylar ignored her questions. Though they had good times together, Madison often annoyed her with her need for attention. She slipped off her shoes, grabbed a soda, and headed for the balcony. She wasn't wasting any of this daytime view, and she still had a couple of hours before needing to go back in to work.

"Things are great here, Sky. I have a new job, my brother-in-law and I are doing better after Ilena's death, and my love life is thriving."

"Great, Madison. Who's the lucky guy?"

"You wouldn't know him. He's not from around here."

"Okay, but what's his name?"

A slight pause.

"Madison?"

"Charles. It's Charles."

"Girl, we do have something for the 'ch' names. Wasn't your last guy a Chris?"

Madison's laughter filled the phone. "No, silly, that was yours."

She was right. Christopher.

"Have you heard from Christopher?" Madison said.

"Just yesterday morning. He called but I didn't answer. Don't know what he wanted." Skylar crossed her leg and opened her bottle of bright red nail polish.

Madison wouldn't like Skylar talking to him. Friends don't let friends do stupid things, Madison always said. To her it would be stupid for Skylar to go back to her husband, the way he'd treated her.

"I don't know what I would say to the man, and I don't really want to find out what he wants. I'm not over it yet, to be honest." Skylar set her phone down and pushed the speakerphone button. "We're coming back in two weeks. Wanna hang out when I'm back?"

"So soon?"

"I've been here over two months already. I love it, but I gotta come back and face my life, Madison. I am adrift in a bed of roses, but even roses need to be watered and nurtured."

"Why don't you stay another couple of months? It won't hurt you. You deserve that much."

"No, we bought the tickets this morning."

Ryan popped his head in. "You want to go out, baby?" he said softly.

She smiled and nodded, held up a finger, then turned back to the phone.

"I'll see you soon, Madison. Enjoy your new man! And congratulations!"

She painted her last two toes and held them up admiringly, reveling in her newfound life and freedom from Christopher. With Ryan life was easy, and she didn't have to worry about anything. She had it good, better than she would have thought possible three months ago.

She reached into her purse and pulled out a green tube. She was getting better at opening these lids. She slid out a wrinkly joint and lit up. Just a few puffs and she'd go. She was more than grateful to Jason for this new and more satisfactory way to calm down and enjoy life. So much more effective than the cold medicine and much simpler than alcohol. This she could handle without getting sick, and she liked herself better when she was chill and relaxed. Christopher was banging that secretary Amanda and likely a couple other women too. That man definitely had problems. She didn't know why she hadn't seen it sooner. But the weed definitely took the sting off of it.

Chapter 3

Raindrops sprinkled on the plastic wrap covering the plate of homemade cookies Madison juggled. The slick key slipped in her fingers. "Damn," she said. The heavy plate chose that moment to slip on the wet fingers of her left hand. She let out a little scream that intensified when a large shadow and a quick hand saved the plate. She whirled around.

"Christopher!" she said, gasping and then blushing.

"You were breaking into my house with a plate of...cookies? That's so sweet..."

"Well, I...I..."

He smiled down at her. "Do you need some help with the lock, dear?" he said.

She blushed deeper at his tease, especially when she saw his eyes linger on her deliberately conspicuous cleavage.

The door flew inward, and Christopher's long arm reached around her and grabbed the curved handle so it didn't slam into the wall. His tattooed arm brushed the side of her face. A whiff of his manly smell made her dizzy. She'd always been attracted to his smell, even way back in school. Too bad Skylar had won him over, but maybe she had a chance now. The man exuded sex appeal like fragrant cedar.

Christopher followed her in and set the plate of cookies down. Could he see her blush? She hazarded a glance at his face. Yes, he had. His eyes bored into hers, and a flush traveled down her neck. His charm disarmed her so much that she found it impossible to not think of her friend's husband "that way"—nor could she look away from his eyes. She knew all about his wandering ways from Skylar, but she didn't seem to have any resistance to him, like always. She tore her eyes away, her feelings equally ragged. With Skylar out of the picture, maybe she would finally have a chance with him, and he would have no need to supplement his desires elsewhere. She would be the perfect wife for him, if given a chance.

"I still had the key Skylar gave me, and since you weren't home, I thought there'd be no harm in leaving these for you."

She and Skylar had been so close that they had exchanged keys, just in case something happened to either of them. Christopher didn't seem upset about it, thankfully.

"I can't believe all the stuff we went through a couple of months ago. How are things going now?"

"I've had better times. And you've had to deal with your sister's death at the hands of that murderer. How are you holding up?"

"Much better now. I could barely come out of my house, let alone my room, for a month. I wish they'd catch the murderer, but from all I know they don't have any leads. Have you heard from Skylar at all?"

"No." He hesitated, then shook his head slightly and left it at that.

"Well, I talked to her this morning and she has two more weeks on the island, then she'll be coming back." Christopher raised his eyebrows slightly, then a cloud covered his face.

"How do you think you're doing now?" she asked.

Christopher pulled the wet plastic wrap from the cookie plate, ignoring the question. "These look good. Snickerdoodles, aren't they? My favorite. How about a hot cup of tea?"

She nodded, still waiting for his answer. He filled the hot water pot and turned it on, then motioned to a chair at the round, retro table with shiny chrome legs and blue vinyl seats. She'd gone with Skylar to pick it out several years before. When he still didn't answer, she said, "Have you thought about what you're going to do about your marriage?"

"We've both been too numb—or preoccupied—to talk about it."

"You look numb, or troubled about something. Is there something else going on?"

Christopher poured the hot water into their mugs, then sat down and watched the steam rise. He finally said, "A woman has contacted me and says her kid is mine. A little girl. Ten years old. Skylar knows about her, but we thought she wasn't pursuing it. We were wrong. The woman is asking for money. Lots of it."

"That's awful for you."

"Yeah. She made a case for retroactive child support with the judge based on the results of the court-ordered paternity test and he ruled in her favor. The man always gets shafted. She won't let me have contact with the girl, either. Her name is Claire."

"What are you going to do?"

"I'll just have to work harder and pay her the money. It isn't right to pay it out of our joint account. Skylar had nothing to do with this. It was before her time. Still, I'm not proud of it."

"You'll get through it. You always have, and you will come out on top of this, too."

"I don't know, Madison. I have more problems than a bird in a hailstorm." He scratched his head and frowned deeper. "I had to let my secretary Amanda go. She is livid and word has it that she wants to sue me for sexual harassment." He shrugged and lowered his head. "I've got something else on my mind, too."

She raised her eyebrows.

"I'm afraid Skylar didn't go to the island alone. I think someone is with her there. I'm just worried she did something foolish, like go off with Steven Quale."

"You mean the murderer? You think she'd do that?"

"Maybe he convinced her he wasn't the one and has some kind of power over her."

Skylar was smart, but Christopher knew how to woo women and sweep them off their feet. How to play with their emotions until they were putty in his hands. He would recognize other men doing it. Some men were naturals, and even though she was aware they were probably acting from a sexual addiction of sorts, she enjoyed the game so much she didn't mind playing around with them.

"Do you really think she'd be that naïve?"

"I wouldn't have thought so, but you never know what's going through someone's head. Everyone has secrets."

Yeah, like his. Madison thanked the universe that she did not have children or a spouse. She relished her freedom from entanglements. They sipped the tea and Christopher reached for her hand. She squeezed his and let hers rest there, enjoying the tingle as his warm hand caressed hers.

Things were going to heat up if she stayed any longer, and with a sudden burst of uncertainty, she stood. "I really need to go now. I have an appointment soon."

Christopher's dubious look caused her to crack a smile, and she raised her eyes to his from under her curly lashes. She couldn't help it. This wouldn't be the end of it, she thought, picking up her purse and keys and smiling at him a bit seductively.

"Hey, do you remember when we went to the antique store in Alexandria? You bought me this." She pulled out an erotic ivory trinket. She'd carried it in her purse for years now. About three inches tall, it was a Japanese couple carved in ivory, two separate figures dressed in traditional Japanese attire with lower halves exposed. When nested together just right, they were engaged in an intimate pastime. They'd had good laughs over it back in the day, and although they'd never quite consummated their relationship, they had both wanted to.

Christopher grinned, his face lighting up. "Yes, ma'am, you bet I do."

She grinned wickedly. She was not as shy as she used to be.

"Stop by any time, Madison. We might as well keep each other company a little, don't you think?"

She sashayed toward the door. *Why not?* She smiled at him, not giving him an answer, then backed out, pulling the door shut behind her.

Chapter 4

The nightclub buzzed with voices and live music. Friday nights at the Martini could always be counted on to be entertaining. Nathaniel Walker had been back from the island for only a day, but he was ready to work. Bartending gave him plenty of interaction with others. His pay was in cash; his pleasure was the quick action of the job. He enjoyed the camaraderie with fellow bartenders, many of whom were women, and with his customers, especially those who tipped well. The good-humored backchat came easy to him. Probably a result of the back-and-forth verbal volleys he'd practiced so much with his foster family and friends all through school.

This enjoyment of his work gave his outgoing alter ego a lot of satisfaction. He could forget about his deficient mother, his favored brother, fake girls, and his dysfunctional childhood while he was working. He knew how to put a good face on things. If he could be who he'd most like to be, it would be this competent, social persona who had no worries and the girl of his dreams at home. But he couldn't see that ever happening now.

Still, he winked at Sasha, the new girl, as she brought him his Gibson martini.

"Hey, I heard you used to bartend here," she said, never slowing. It took only a moment for him to see she was good. She was also easy on the eyes, with her shiny black hair twisted into a bun on the back of her head. Sexy.

"Yup."

"When you comin' back?"

"Don't know. Soon, though."

"It'll be good to have you," she said, glancing cautiously around her.

Problems? He could deal with that.

"You married?" he asked. She had a single ring on her ring finger, but it wasn't a diamond and didn't look like a traditional wedding band.

She stopped her constant motion, her gaze leveling on him directly. She didn't say anything, but her silence was a warning for him to back off. He held up both hands.

"Hey, no reason to get defensive there," he said.

"You should know yourself how it is for a female in this business. Don't make those mistakes."

He'd have to watch it with this one. She was top notch. The familiar tightening sensation came, a sharp and piercing pain and longing inside his chest, this time stronger than ever.

She moved behind the bar with precision and grace, every movement controlled and executed to maximize her efficiency. He enjoyed watching her. She reminded him of Daischa, his foster sister, the only girl who fully accepted him just as he was. Daischa used to tell him his physical characteristics from his mixed parentage looked attractive on him. His medium skin tones with his spiky blond hair and striking blue eyes made him stand out, and he didn't like to stand out. But her kind comments had done wonders for his confidence.

"Hey, Nathaniel!" A hand clamped down on his shoulder. "You back in town to stay?"

He knew that voice without even turning. The false cheerfulness. He flinched, then grimaced. Cecil, the manipulative bastard. Why couldn't his mother's disgusting brother find another bar to hang out at? No doubt the know-it-all had come to stir up trouble, like always. The man's shirt stretched across his belly and barely covered his waist.

Nathaniel shrugged off the hand and turned, his icy eyes locking with his uncle's dark ones. The sour smell of booze oozed from the man's pores, the alcoholism a disease that ran through the family. His mother had a problem with substance abuse too, and Nathaniel thanked the powers that be that he did not inherit that weakness. He was not weak like her or his stepbrother Christopher, who could not control his impulses with women. Thank God she hadn't coddled him, even as a toddler, like she did Christopher. In that way he was thankful to have grown up in his foster home, far removed from her clutches. Daischa, his foster sister, had been his saving grace. He missed her but was loath to involve her any more in his miserable life, and the breakup had been and still was difficult. She loved him only because she didn't know all of him.

Realizing Cecil had been jabbering about his sister Bobbie, Nathaniel's mother, he tuned back in, his anger rising. There was no name he detested more than hers. But he could not risk his anger leaking out here in the bar. He spoke quietly, yet with cold vitriol.

"Cecil, if I could, I'd smash that nose of yours into your face to get you out of mine. Get out of my sight." The flashback of this moron looking on with a smirk on his face while his sister beat her young son because she hated the boy's father nearly caused him to lose the control he had long fought for. He'd never forgotten the man's cruelty in all the years in foster care. He'd been about six years old at the time, and soon after, his mother was kicked out of the rental and had abandoned him. He was out on the street, and he swore from that moment on, even at such a tender age, that he would tell no one her name. But he'd never forgotten, and she hadn't gone far. Over the years he'd spent plenty of time watching from his secluded hiding spot in the bushes of the empty lot across the street. Cecil lived in the run-down trailer home two doors down. Brother and sister had fallen from the same diseased apple tree.

A face flashed before his eyes—the man's worthless daughter Briana. Beautiful girl, but he'd never been interested. He'd heard Briana had gotten married a year ago, but the rumors were that she was already running around on him. Why get married at all if you weren't going to be faithful? He didn't get it. If only Daischa...but he just couldn't. She'd get hurt.

The beat of the music pulsed around him. Caught up in his thoughts, he didn't see the fist coming at him.

His head snapped to the side and rage filled him.

Nathaniel came back at Cecil with a punch designed to connect with the man's jaw, but Cecil feinted to the side. Nathaniel, being taller, stronger, younger, and undoubtedly smarter, kicked the bar stool out from under him. Cecil went down. Nathaniel restrained his anger. This wasn't how he wanted things to go. Better Cecil get in trouble than him, so he held himself back.

"You punk!" Cecil jumped up, fists swinging. Nathaniel dodged again. He looked over to the bouncer at the door who knew him well and was watching. Nathaniel gave a small tilt of his head toward Cecil, who noticed the nonverbal cues he'd sent to Bruce. The disgusting lowlife sputtered, drops of saliva visible in the air in front of him.

"I shoulda joined in the fun when Bobbie gave you a thrashin', you dickhead. Your father was scum and you look just like him!"

Bruce made his way past several tables of people, all of whom had tuned in to the fight that Nathaniel never allowed to get off the ground. Bruce grabbed Cecil's shirt from the back and told him it was time for him to leave. He hoped Bruce would tell Cecil not to come back.

Nathaniel didn't need any more reminders of how much he hated his mother and her family. He had put up with far too much from all of them. His only consolation was his relationships with Ryan and Daischa. If his mom hadn't abandoned him and let the state put him in foster care, he'd never have met either Ryan or Daischa. They were all victims. He could count on his friend, the only pseudo-brother who mattered. Ryan, who understood his anger and seemed to have little problem with his leisure activities, or at least the little he knew of them, and who looked the other way, giving Nathaniel the freedom to work things out himself. Nathaniel appreciated his support, yet he purposely used—or abused—Ryan's natural goodhearted nature. Ryan was sensitive, warm, and soft, and therefore easy to take advantage of.

Yes, he needed to put this behind him and try again to shake off his hideously dysfunctional life as soon as possible. He'd been thinking about making a new start in Jamaica and running his business from there. If only he could start a brand-new life and find some inner peace. But that didn't seem likely.

He smiled, taking a little satisfaction from the fact that he was getting away with the surveillance. He'd been casing his mother's house and activities for years and had fantasized, more times than he was comfortable admitting, about what he would do if he had half the chance. Something always held him back—something base—as though there were something even more intrinsically wrong with harming one's own biological mother than some other female. But she'd get what was coming to her eventually.

Chapter 5

Skylar had gotten the news when she and Ryan were going through airport security. Christopher had texted again, and she called him back. His niece, Briana, was dead. Although she had lived for over a week following the house fire, she had not survived, and the authorities called it murder. Yet they had no evidence to point to a killer.

Now here she stood, nose-to-nose with the last person she'd wanted to see at the girl's funeral.

"Christopher. How nice to see you again."

"Hey, Sky. How was your time out of the country?"

Was the man actually being polite? Friendly? What was up with that?

"It's going to take me some time to settle back in. I'm not going back to counseling, so I'm working on starting something different. Meanwhile, I'll work at the department store." She regretted not bringing Madison with her to the funeral, but her friend claimed she was still too distraught over her sister Ilene's murder. Besides, she had a date to prepare for.

The killer had escaped the day Detective Shannon Short shot herself, and he was still at large, with most of the city still on alert, and women everywhere fearful they'd be his next victim, including her. This time the victim had been Christopher's cousin, his Uncle Cecil's daughter, and even though the girl was no good, it was still pretty scary. These murders just kept happening, too close for anyone's comfort.

Skylar realized her nerves were making her too talkative, but she couldn't help herself. "Law enforcement must have some idea whether this murder can be linked to the others. Have you heard anything about that?"

Christopher nodded. "Yes, they found the letter 'A' on her belly, just like the others. Why they can't get anywhere on this is the bigger mystery."

"If the 'A' truly means adultery, all the women killed were guilty of it, and Briana is no exception, as everyone knows. And many more adulterous women are living in fear." She shuddered visibly, drawing inside herself, realizing that she, too, fit that description, technically. If she had half a chance, she'd ask the killer what he had against women. Why wasn't he killing adulterous men too? She looked back at her husband. His expression had grown serious.

He seemed different, but she had no idea what to make of it. Was he humbler? Time would tell. She didn't know if she wanted to have anything more to do with him. She could barely look at him anymore. And Ryan was giving her all she needed at the moment. They'd only been back for a few days, but she could see herself staying with him indefinitely. He seemed to like having her there, and he always treated her well. So well that it made it hard to think of leaving him.

"Do you want to sit with me?" Christopher asked, a bit hesitant.

"No, I'm not ready for that. Thanks anyway," she said, her heart twisting a little inside.

"Well, let's talk again soon. We have a lot of decisions to make between us." He hesitated, clearly wanting to say more. She lifted an eyebrow and he opened his mouth, stuttering over the words.

"I'm s—"

"No." She shook her head. He was going to apologize, and she didn't want to hear it or be on the spot to say something in return.

Christopher's pained look told her more than she wanted to think about. It told her he was becoming remorseful. And she had no idea how she'd respond to that. Better to just ignore it for now. She would have to be careful talking to him, because she didn't want him to know too much about what she was doing. Where she was staying, for starters. She'd have to hurry and make some money so she could get her own place. Ryan was great, but until she had her marriage figured out, she was going to need some space.

As she entered the sanctuary, she saw Cecil with Christopher's mother Bobbie on the front row. Their heads were lowered, but she couldn't bring herself to feel sorry for them after all the things Christopher had told her about his mother. The woman had neglected him while at the same time doting on him and holding him up as an example of what a son should be. He'd become ambitious for himself because of her neglect and false praise. She was great at guilt trips, when in reality her status-seeking behavior was pitiful.

In Skylar's opinion, the woman deserved no credit whatsoever for the good in Christopher. She was the primary cause of

Christopher's womanizing because of her poor example and bad parenting, and it was hard to see that he got any of his charm or good looks from her. The woman deserved to have some bad feelings after all she'd done to hurt her sons—or all her children—but Skylar doubted she had a conscience. Skylar hadn't heard anything about Nathaniel, Christopher's stepbrother, for quite some time, and knew next to nothing about his younger siblings. Where had his stepbrother Nathaniel been all these years? Even Christopher had no clue. Skylar didn't know what he looked like and wouldn't be able to recognize him on the street.

As Skylar suffered through the short service on the back row, she battled with her desire to see what all she could learn versus leaving directly after the service. Funerals could be entertaining, as long as you weren't the one grieving. She had no intention of going to the graveside. She'd signed the guest book and that would have to be enough. Maybe she'd just stick around for a quick bite to eat at the reception, given generously by the church's good-hearted women who had no clue who these non-churchgoing people were. She'd say a quick word to Christopher's family even though her stomach was tied up in knots, especially after seeing her husband again. He sure looked fine to her, but that's as far as she was willing to let her feelings go.

The short service ended with the last note of a standard funeral hymn and she rose and headed to the narthex, yanking on her tight skirt to straighten it, then she headed down the stairs.

Christopher's other siblings stood against the wall, chatting quietly. The only other one she knew at all and could stand, Cinda, detached herself and came to greet her.

"I can't believe you braved coming out to this shit-show, Skylar," she began. "If I weren't a part of this family, I wouldn't be here."

"I don't know why I'm here, truthfully. Maybe because Christopher and I are still married, and I feel some kind of obligation—"

"That brother of mine has been the devil in a number of women's lives, I'm afraid, not just yours." Cinda's bitterness toward her own family was notable.

"I'm sick of seeing these murders," Skylar said. "They are affecting people all around me, and that is not acceptable. Any of us could be the next target."

"I need to tell you something. I don't know if it's significant or not, but it's strange. You know Nathaniel, don't you? Our half-brother? The one Mother lost when she was kicked out of her apartment years ago?"

"Yes. I have never met him that I know of."

"Well, maybe you don't know, but he bartends over at the Martini. Haven't you seen him? Tall, fit, buzz-cut blond hair and blue eyes?"

"That good looking guy is Nathaniel? I have spoken with him before, but I had no clue he was related."

"He's a little strange. I first saw him when I was just a little girl. I was outside playing one day, and I saw a kid across the street, slipping into the big bushes in the front yard. Those evergreen bushes have room inside around their trunks where a person could sit completely undetected. But I've seen him in there a bunch of times because I notice things. I think he sat there and watched the house. Who knows why, poor kid."

"When do you remember seeing him last?"

Cinda lifted her paper cup of coffee to her mouth, blowing on the steam, eyeing the varieties of cake on individual paper plates. "You want a piece?" she said, not answering the question. Skylar nodded. She'd been eyeing them since she entered the room and was glad to have a chance to indulge her sweet tooth. They both chose a chocolate layer cake heavy with frosting. It was always time for comfort food.

As they walked side-by-side to the long tables, Cinda said, "I remember it vividly. I was getting out of my date's car about six months ago and I saw a little flash of light from the bushes. I have no doubt it was him. The flashlight was on, but it was too dark to see his face. After I went in, I watched from the front window until the light went out and a tall figure emerged from the back of the bushes, the streetlight illuminating his short blond hair. He crept across the driveway and down the street. Why he's still watching now that he's a grown man is very strange. Don't you think?"

Cecil had moved away from the tight group around his sister Bobbie, and he approached them, a smirk on his face.

"So, it's the womanizing husband's counterpart. How ya doing, Skylar?" He licked his already wet lips, a disgusting habit, she thought.

"You're a disgrace." Skylar looked down her nose at him.

Unfazed, he continued his obnoxiousness. "What are you two conniving about over here? I hope you're sharing ideas as to who this madman is who keeps wiping out the lives of these innocent young women."

"No disrespect, but we'd prefer you move on." Skylar had no qualms about returning the man's rudeness. She doubted he was in any distress over his own daughter's death, and that steamed her.

"You are at my daughter's funeral, Ms. Skylar. Condolences are in order." He turned slightly and stuck out his stubbled cheek, trawling for a kiss.

"Grow up, you lech. Leave us alone."

Cecil made an obscene gesture. Skylar turned her back in time to see Christopher headed intentionally for them. Great. She didn't need him defending her here, but once he stood next to her, she was glad for it. He stared Cecil down and the man moved off. She turned to Christopher and gave him a grateful look.

"Thanks," she said.

He nodded, his expression somber. Skylar took a bite of the cake and offered one to him. He shook his head, clearly not enjoying himself.

As the tension stretched out, she finished her last bite and said, "I've got to go." She swiveled, making a beeline for the staircase. When she reached its safety, she swiped at her wet eyes. What was up with her? Maybe being near Christopher was affecting her more than she thought. A ball of confused anger churned inside. How could she feel anything for him after all he'd done?

She stood outside the church's heavy wooden doors. The wind whipped her hair and made her shiver. She hadn't heard Christopher come out, but there he was again, standing near her. Too near. She moved a few steps away, then turned to him. It had been a mistake to come.

"I don't want you, Christopher," she said, the words tearing up her voice as they forced their way out. "I don't want to talk to you."

She didn't look at him again, and eventually he moved away while she fought her tears. How many women had he messed around with and who were they? Only he knew. Maybe even with her best friend Madison.

She started down the short flight of stairs, catching a glimpse of a familiar face. In the passenger seat of a late-model Honda sedan sat her former client and county coroner, Vesta. In the driver's seat sat a uniformed officer. He was not too old, but he was big and looked pretty tough. She nodded at them. They were here to do their jobs, watchful for any suspicious activities that could provide clues on apprehending a murderer. This new killing would bring in more law enforcement. She should arrange a time to speak with Vesta soon. The woman might know things that Skylar could use to help her stay safe.

Chapter 6

Madison answered on the first ring. "How was it?" Skylar said.

"Terrible. I ran into Christopher, who I didn't want to talk to, but it was unavoidable. I was the first one out the door." Madison was unusually quiet for once.

"You okay, Madison?"

"Yes, I guess so. It's just hard to think about. Sometimes I feel okay and other times this intense anger takes over and all I want to do is lash out at something or someone."

"That's okay. You're still going through the stages of grief. You remember them, don't you? They don't always follow a distinct pattern. You could be bouncing around between anger and depression and not made it through to the acceptance stage yet."

"How the hell long does it take, Sky? I'm tired of this. I find myself looking for things that will distract me or pacify me, sometimes in an unhealthy way. Nothing seems worth doing. Why can't they catch this guy? It's a good thing I have a job to go to, otherwise I'd stay in bed."

"I hear you. You've got to give it the time it takes. You know, Christopher seemed different today."

"How so?"

"Well, just quiet. Reserved. Humble."

"I probably shouldn't say anything, but you might want to know he has had some contact with some woman from his past. She wants money. And—well, I shouldn't say."

"When did you find this out? Did you see Christopher while I was gone?"

More hesitation. Something was definitely off with her friend.

"Yes, I baked one day and thought it would feel good to reach out and do something nice for someone, so I took him some of the extra cookies. He told me about Lisa and his daughter."

"That woman is calling him again?"

"I—I've said too much. He should be the one to tell you what's going on."

"That's not fair, Madison. I'm inclined to let this go since you've been grieving, but first, I'm not real excited you went to see him, and second, to find out she hasn't dropped this."

"I think I'll bow out now and let you talk to Christopher about it. If it helps any, I too noticed a change in him."

"Okay. Thanks for telling me, Madison. I'll get the rest from Christopher." She sat in Ryan's double-wide recliner, the only cushy piece of furniture in his condo. Everything else was modern—clean, simple, and neutral—all designed to show off the art displayed at every turn.

What had Madison and Christopher been up to while she'd been gone? Disgusted by the thought, she got up and fixed herself a cup of coffee in the French press. She didn't want either of them to know where she was staying. She didn't think either knew she'd been with Ryan, and that's how she wanted to keep it.

Skylar had left a few loose ends with her counseling business. When she and Ryan left for the Virgin Islands, she'd packed and stored most of her boxes in Ryan's locked storage unit. This condo provided storage units in an enclosed area in the parking lot, just a short walk from the back entrance. She had brought several boxes inside the day before. Ryan said he'd be leaving in the morning and would be gone for a few days, and she relished the thought of having a nice place to stay and some time to herself to sort things out and make plans.

The modern condo had an artist's flair that drew her in, and she spent an hour perusing the pieces of art Ryan had collected from around the world. She stood in front of each piece trying to understand what the artist was attempting to convey, but art appreciation wasn't really her thing. The appreciating seemed like a lot of effort.

As she stood in front of a particularly colorful piece of art in the stairwell he called "cubism" and that made no sense at all to her, Coco, Ryan's African parrot, squawked out a sexy wolf whistle. Then he said, "Whatcha doing? Give me a kiss." The bird was cute, no doubt about it, but annoying as heck. He went with the décor, with his distinct black and white markings and his gray body. When Coco was out of his cage, he could camouflage well with the stark, modern surroundings.

Stir crazy and not knowing when Ryan would be back, she decided to go out and find something to do, even if it was just to shop without buying anything. She needed a job. A lot of things were in limbo, and the money she had saved up in her account would not last forever. She wrote Ryan a quick note and hurried out the door, glad to escape Coco's loud squawking. She'd have to talk to Christopher soon. She got in the car and took a moment to send Vesta a message. She had things to find out in relation to the latest murder. It had hit too close to home. What was the body count up to? First one she knew about was the woman they called Misty, then Ilena, Madison's sister, and now Briana, Christopher's cousin. Who would the killer target next? Assuming it was the same killer?

Chapter 7

Ryan closed the front door and stood in the dark, silent condo. Where was Skylar? In the kitchen, he picked up a handwritten note that sat under the corner of a pan of brownies. *Out for the evening. Won't be late. ~Sky*

Where could she have gone? Maybe she was shopping. Hoping he'd have some time to think, he poured himself a whiskey and sat in the recliner. His run-in with Nathaniel at the bar the night before had not gone well. He'd stopped in for a quick drink on his way home and found Nathaniel working again. His foster brother had tried to strong-arm him into helping him cover his tracks for some nefarious, cryptic deed again and Ryan resented it and had refused. Sure, they'd had a bond, but Ryan wanted a normal, happy life now that he was out of foster care and had some good experiences behind him with his art. His business was going well, and he hoped things would work out with Skylar. Surely she wouldn't go back to her playboy husband now. He thought he'd done a good job of giving her what she needed. At least she seemed to like making love with him, and he knew he was giving her quality time.

He opened his tablet and looked over the list of his art dealings, trying to focus on which sales to prioritize, but he couldn't shake his unease about Nathaniel. The guy was a mystery. Just what was he thinking in his spare time? Why was he targeted by the police like he was? Surely he couldn't be murdering young women...could he? Detective Short had seemed to think the killer had a connection to this condo, like it was registered to someone with the killer's alias, but now she was gone, her suicide having left everyone in shock, even him. It was time for Ryan to think about separating himself from Nathaniel as much as possible, starting with moving out of this condo. It might take him a month or so, but that's what he'd do. Watch and distance himself. He could no longer ignore Nathaniel's apparent dark side.

Just two weeks ago, Nathaniel had left him the set of sheets on the island. They were a nice design, with pink rosebuds, and had a good thread count. He'd washed them and put them on Skylar's bed. She liked how he did these nice things for her comfort, so he hadn't wasted any time in using the sheets. The gift had been a nice gesture. His mind worked hard, trying to understand his foster brother. Nathaniel had done well with his business. His main facility was close by, and his second one, his design studio, was on the island. Ryan's instincts were to cut loose of him, the sooner the better. He'd ignored his gut feelings too long. He gathered his dreads into a bunch and put them loosely into a leather hair scrunchy.

His condo had three bedrooms, one of which he'd given to Skylar so she could feel like she had her own space. He needed his, too. But most nights she was in his bed, and they both liked that. She'd gotten used to his peculiarities, one of which was that he'd often get up during the night and move about, staying up sometimes until morning, but often slipping back into bed before the day began. He needed the time alone as much as he needed her. He moved from his chair, grabbed a glass of water from the kitchen, and climbed the staircase to the upper level, where the open hallway looked over the open space of the living and dining rooms below.

As he stood looking, the front door burst open. He'd forgotten to lock it. He startled, dropping his glass of water. Nathaniel stood in the doorway, the porch light shining in and illuminating him from behind, his spiky blond hair longer than Ryan remembered, the mess of it highlighted by the glow and casting a wild shadow on the far wall.

The guy always seemed larger than life, and this time was no exception. He exuded repressed energy, or some kind of hostility, and Ryan did not fully understand him, though he'd tried to be a friend to help Nathaniel deal with his inner demons. But he always got the feeling deep down that he was being used.

"Hey, how's it going? You could've knocked." He projected his voice from the upper walkway, not sure if Nathaniel was able to see him in the shadows. Strong negative vibes projected from him tonight, and he tensed at the sound of Nathaniel's voice.

"When did you get back?" Nathaniel said, snapping out the words.

"Couple days ago."

"Where's Skylar?"

"She's out. She left a note but didn't say where she was going. Why?"

"You going to stay with her? What's going on between her and her rotten husband?"

"Why are you so interested in her, Nathaniel? Why are you here asking questions about her?"

Ryan hadn't seen this mood from Nathaniel in a long time, and it made him uneasy. His mind flashed back to another time Nathaniel's temper had been ignited, some years ago now. Nathaniel had violated Ryan's sense of justice by an act of violence against Daischa, their foster sister, over her little yapping dog. Ryan had come to her defense, which had pissed Nathaniel off. The coldness that oozed from him tonight triggered Ryan, tired as he was of dealing with Nathaniel and getting nowhere. Maybe he should calm the guy down and send him on his way in a hurry before Skylar returned.

"You know, you have a lot of nerve barging in here and grilling me about Skylar. Why do you care, man?" He descended the stairs until he stepped onto the porcelain tile of the entry floor. They were fifteen feet apart and Nathaniel's posture had not changed, nor had he moved inside. The front door was still open behind him, the streetlight behind him making it difficult to see Nathaniel's face. Thunder rumbled in the distance.

They locked eyes, Ryan meeting his old buddy's icy blue ones with matching intensity. He had a few inches of height on him. He remembered the standoff from the past like it had been yesterday. Ryan had come into foster care as a toddler, and their foster family had been a relatively stable one. He'd toed the line and had appreciated the structure of the home, while Nathaniel had a wild streak in him and bent and broke the rules over and over. Still, Ryan had sensed the pain inside of the younger boy and had always wanted to do something that would make a difference for Nathaniel, but he was so filled with bitterness.

The moment lengthened and though Nathaniel did not lower his eyes, he did break contact first, turning his head to look outside as a crash of thunder sounded, closer now.

"You're better off sending her back to her husband. She'll go back to him anyway, you know. They always do. And then they'll repeat their whoring with someone else. Just drop her, Ryan. It's for the best."

Ryan wasn't going to let anyone tell him what to do where Skylar was concerned. She was becoming his, whether she realized it or not. She wouldn't go back. Would she?

"Why do you care, Nathaniel?"

"You've always had it easy, bro. You got the girls, and you had it better than me with our foster family. They actually liked you. Yeah, you're my brother. Just like my other brother, Christopher. The one our mother always favored."

"Listen to me now, bro," Ryan said. "You have to stop playing the victim in your life. The past is the past. It is over. You have everything you need to make a good life and all you have to do is get off your soapbox of revenge and start living it."

"Oh, it's just so easy, isn't it. Everyone has it easy but me."

"Not true. You have everything in place to make yourself a good life. You're a great bartender, you're good-looking, and you have the intelligence to set goals for yourself and your life. Why are you stuck in the past? We have to leave that shit behind. We know what a good life looks like. Hell, that's all we used to think about. We can make that life for ourselves now. Go to therapy. It'll help."

"I have no money for that."

Nathaniel's face had darkened, either a sign of anger or hurt. Ryan needed to get him to leave.

"Go now and make a plan as to how to improve your life, then carry it out. Just do your best. I know you can do it."

"Yeah, I can do that. Thanks so much, *brother*." He rolled the last word out with heavy sarcasm.

"Come on, Nathaniel. Don't resent me. Find a way to let go of your bitterness. No one can give you a better life except you." Ryan moved closer, hoping Nathaniel would become calm enough that he could touch him. Maybe not a hug, but at least a human touch on the arm or shoulder.

Nathaniel took a step back. "You are an arrogant son of a bitch, Ryan. How dare you tell me what to do."

"What's happened to you, Nathaniel? You seem like you've gotten into some kind of business that's not doing you any good."

"Just shut the hell up, Ryan." Nathaniel's face contorted.

"Arrr," Coco the parrot said, his sailor talk coming upon him. Ryan swung his head to the side, realizing he'd left the bird out of his cage. He didn't see the fist coming at his face, but Coco did. The fist landed on Ryan's jaw. Coco swooped off the cage and shot toward the duo. Nathaniel didn't see or hear him until he caught sight of the bird in his peripheral vision. His arm flew up and slammed into the bird, but not before a claw swept across his forehead and a thin line of blood formed, spreading out quickly and dripping into his eye as the bird dropped to the floor. His eyes were open, but he wasn't moving.

"Get out of my house!" Ryan roared.

Nathaniel wiped his forehead, smearing the blood, then turned on his heel and exited, but not before growling out, "You'll get what's coming to you, *brother*."

Chapter 8

Skylar pulled into the parking spot that always seemed to be open just for her. The mystery of the open parking space must be a sign she was meant to be here with Ryan. She smiled. The man could always soothe her with his voice and his words. He had a beautiful way of expressing himself, and the kindest heart she'd ever seen in a man. Was she falling in love with him? She had no clue what love was anymore. But she was happy with him.

Rain pummeled her, and lightning struck nearby, the resulting thunder following so closely she knew she needed to make a run for it. She swept through the cracked doorway and was astonished to see Ryan sitting in his chair, holding Coco in his lap, a huge bump on his jawline. He was cooing softly to the bird.

"What happened?" she said, hurrying over.

Ryan looked up, eyes wet and tortured. "Is he okay, baby? What happened? How'd he get hurt?" She lay her hand on his shoulder and bent down to look at the bird closely. His eyes were open, but he wasn't moving at all. "Is he—"

"No, he's breathing. He's been looking at me like this for fifteen minutes now."

Ryan could barely get the words out. He'd had the bird for ten years. Barely a teenager in parrot years.

When Coco caught sight of Skylar, he struggled, then jumped to his feet. He blinked a few times and then squawked out, "Whatcha doin', sweetie? Give me a kiss!"

They both broke into wide smiles, cooing and laughing along with the bird, who seemed to have regained his mojo. "Well, he seems to really have a thing for you, Skylar."

"How did he get hurt?" she repeated.

"I opened the door to look out at the storm and he came from behind. I think he was going to land on my shoulder, but instead the door hit him."

"Then how'd you get that knot on your jaw? It looks like it's going to be quite a bruise."

"After the door hit Coco, I tripped and fell into the edge of the door."

"You must have felt terrible after all that. But I'm so glad I could revive Coco," she said, smiling.

"You're the best. Let's give him a treat and get to bed. My room tonight?" he said.

She winked, then poured them each a glass of milk and set a couple of plates in front of the brownies. Coco sat on Ryan's shoulder, and neither felt like enforcing the rule of no birds at the table. Coco played with Ryan's dreads, sifting them through his beak.

"I'm planning to move soon," Ryan said. "I know we just got back, but I don't feel comfortable here anymore, what with the things that have been going on. You know...the chance that this place is registered in the name of the murderer. Although how that came to pass, I haven't a clue."

"What about your foster brother? I thought he owned it."

"Nathaniel?"

"Yeah, he's the bartender down at the Martini. Right?"

"Yes, he does own this place, but for some reason Detective Short thought this 'Steven Quale' owned it. Haven't figured that out yet. I'm afraid Nathaniel has secrets. You remember, when Detective Short discovered I wasn't the killer, she roped me into playing a role for her and bringing your husband in at gunpoint? I didn't tell you, but she was furious about her pregnancy and was a little out of her mind. I figured my best course of action was to go along with her."

"Well, I'm going to talk to the coroner who was a former patient of mine. Vesta. Maybe she will tell me what evidence they have now. I saw her and the new detective—Tommy Little, I think—in the patrol car watching the church after Briana's funeral."

"This has all been exhausting. Let's go to bed." Ryan rose from the chair, Coco not leaving his shoulder. He moved to the door, locking it and giving it an extra tug for good measure. Then he went to the closet and retrieved his three-pronged steel security bar with rubber stoppers on the ends, something he'd ordered before they left for the island. Now was the time to use it.

"You think we need that tonight?"

"I'm just a little nervous, I guess. I think it's time we use it every time we are home. With everything that's going on, we can't be too safe or careful. I want you to think about that whenever you're here. I'll work on getting us a different place, one not owned by Nathaniel, where we can be happy and not afraid."

The whistled opening of Bobby McFerrin's song burst out of the head-bobbing gray bird, followed closely by the lyrics. *"Don't worry...be happyyy."* They laughed in unison.

After putting the bird to bed in his cage with a new treat, Ryan patted Skylar's behind, and she wiggled it for him. "Let's go," he said.

She smiled.

Chapter 9

Skylar entered the gate of the botanical gardens and waved at Vesta, who was sitting on the bench in the lobby of the facility. Her face wore a frown.

"Why the sad face, Vesta?" Skylar flung her thin red scarf back over her shoulder. She'd only visited the gardens in the spring, when flowers were in bloom. It would be interesting to see it in September, but what she was most interested in was what Vesta would tell her about the case. The woman had come to see Skylar six months ago for therapy after not being able to handle her sadness after her divorce. They'd enjoyed each other's company, and when the murder of Madison's sister occurred, Vesta's care and concern had been a comfort. She had a mother's touch.

"Chile, you know I got my hands full right now. These murders are weighing me down. You did good to suggest this place to meet. Let's get walking. We could both use the exercise."

Skylar grinned and they started off down the wide path. Blue hydrangeas were in bloom, and the fall colors set them off beautifully.

"You still doing counseling, Skylar?" Vesta asked.

"No ma'am, I just got back from being away on the island. I've got to find a job, and soon."

"You not doing therapy anymore?" she shrieked. "You really helped me."

"I've got my sights set on doing mentoring for women. Specifically, relationship coaching."

"Ambitious."

"Well, I'm not ready to do it yet. I need a little training, and I need to also get my own life put back together. But it'll come."

"What are you going to do about Christopher?"

"I don't know, Vesta. I saw him at the funeral. He looked good, but...I just won't be able to trust him again. He's not going to change his stripes."

"You don't seem too upset. You didn't find no islander to take up with while you were gone, did you?"

Skylar smiled. Vesta tried to catch her eye, but she kept her head turned and changed the subject.

"So," Skylar said, "I was hoping you might fill me in as much as you can on what you're doing on the case. To tell you the truth, I'm a bit scared, but not too much. I'm keeping my eyes wide open and a security bar on my door."

"And you should. This guy is as slippery as a seal. He's got too many successful murders behind him. He's smart. Careful. And he may have help."

"Oh? Why do you think so?"

"Here, sit," Vesta said, motioning to a wooden bench with a memorial plaque on one side. "The only clue we have, and you're going to laugh—"

"What is it?"

"A single pill. You'll never guess."

"Out with it already!" Skylar said.

"It's Staxyn."

"Vesta! I don't know what that is."

"Staxyn is a medication in the same family as Levitra. I will assume you aren't familiar with these. They treat erectile dysfunction."

"ED? You've got to be kidding." It took a second for the significance to kick in. She burst out with an unenthusiastic laugh, like she wasn't sure whether it was laughable. "So, the killer raped and killed all these women by using Staxyn? Is that what you're saying?"

"Not exactly. Crazy thing is, none of these women were raped. They were, however, sexually aroused."

"Oh, wow. What a clue. Kinda useless, but it is a clue."

"I gave Detective Little the pill I found to put with the other evidence, but I remembered the characteristics of the pill and that is what I found out."

"Anything else?"

"Yeah. A couple of things. First, the telltale letter 'A.' And it appeared that the set of sheets used was one the killer brought with him. They were pink and had flowers on them. We can't find the company that makes them. The sheets had no labels. No one had cut the labels off; they just were never there to begin with. The company made them without labels."

"Sheets? You mean, it's his new signature? I thought there were sheets with flowers on them in the very first murder, too."

"Oh, there were enough similarities that we believe he is one and the same."

"Let's keep walking," Skylar said, nervous energy making her skittish. They continued around the Koi pond and stopped a moment to admire the huge waterlilies.

"Honey, you need to be careful now. Very careful. You could be in his sights."

Skylar glanced at her sideways. Did the woman think she was unfaithful? Of course she did.

"We believe this killer wants to be found. If he didn't, he'd be more careful who he targets and would likely have a broader scope, although there have been recent serial killings that have no suspects. All of this is being looked at. The other consideration is that he's trying to relieve his inner anguish by targeting women who are like someone who wronged him. Serial killing can be a retaliatory act of sorts. He probably has a psychosis as well and is likely to be either a 'visionary' type or a 'mission' type. The visionary targets specific groups of individuals and is compelled by voices or visions, and they don't necessarily understand why they are doing it. They have psychotic breaks. The mission type feels a need or duty to target certain classes of people such as prostitutes. Just keep these things in mind."

"That's not very reassuring, Vesta." Skylar walked faster, arms swinging.

"You need to carry something for protection, honey. Do you have anything?"

"No, I have never felt unsafe before."

"Go online and at least order some pepper spray. See what else is available and make sure you could use it if necessary. Don't think you can just kick him in the nuts, okay?"

Skylar gave her a wry smile. "Tell me about the new detective. Is he any good?"

"Tommy Little? Yes. He's a ball of fire. But this is a high-profile investigation now. The FBI is all over it. This killer better watch his step, that's all I have to say. Still, you make yourself safe, girl."

They reached the building, hit up the drinking fountain, and headed for their vehicles.

"Make sure you watch your car. Any place someone could accost you, you need to be watching."

"Okay, will do. Thanks for your help!"

"Sure, and I hope to join your mentoring group when you get it up and running. I could use some support."

"I will let you know. I could use a good client or two to get started, so that will be great. But it's a ways off. I have to get things settled with Christopher first."

They waved and smiled, and Skylar headed back to the condo. She needed to look for her own place soon, so she kept her eyes open for acceptable townhouses as she drove.

Skylar reached the condo. She was looking forward to finishing her second Stephen King book and starting a new one, with a cup of hot tea in hand. Chai, of course, her favorite. She walked toward the kitchen and heard a voice whisper, "You'll get what's coming to you, *brother*." She froze, turning her head carefully to look into the shadowy corners of the room. All she could see was the bird, who swung quietly in his large cage.

"Coco? Did you hear that?" she asked. The bird gazed at her for a moment, then squawked out his typical greeting for her, a wolf whistle and a "Whatcha doing? Give me a kiss."

She'd have to ask Ryan about the strange words. She texted him, asking when he'd be back.

"Not until late," he replied. "I have dinner with a client and then we're going back to his place to talk business."

She sighed, glad his trip had been postponed another day, then she barred the door. A long, soaking bath was out of the question tonight.

Chapter 10

Skylar tried to focus. This fear of the murderer was taking over her life. Not only could she not decide what she ought to do next, she also couldn't sleep. Ryan had come home at ten o'clock the night before and he seemed as confused as she was about the whispering voice. He'd considered it might be Coco who said it, but why would he? It made no sense. And the way the voice said "brother," drawled as if a threat...what could that mean, if anything?

She tripped over the wheel of her suitcase and swore. She could at least put the thing away. It had been sitting out ever since they got back from the island. Pulling out the remaining items, her hand encountered something hard. Before it registered, she'd lifted it out and looked at it. The framed photo of her and Christopher, smiling and happy, the first picture she had of them together, did not make her smile. It made her angry. Suddenly, her desire for revenge by infidelity was gone. Still, there was Ryan. She turned the picture upside down on the dresser and finished unpacking, shoving things into the empty dresser drawers, her natural orderliness succumbing to her sudden painful, turbulent feelings.

She looked over the railing to the kitchen below. Ryan was cleaning the bird cage. He'd be leaving soon. Coco waddled on the counter, muttering the word "brother," with first one inflection, then another. She was so absorbed in watching, she hadn't realized her sock was wet.

"Ryan, why is it wet up here?" she hollered.

"Sorry, I spilled my water. Guess it hasn't dried yet."

Ryan was the easiest man she'd ever known to get along with. Calm, easygoing, spontaneous, good-hearted. She had no problems with his personal habits. He practiced yoga and meditation regularly. Where he got the self-discipline from, she didn't know, but she was envious. He lived his life simply and authentically, and she usually felt very calm around him. It would be almost effortless to stay with him.

Her confusion angered her. Returning to the bedroom, she slipped into her open-back sneakers and grabbed the picture, then galloped down the stairs. "I'm going out to the storage room. I need to put this out there." She held up the picture for him to see. He gave her an understanding smile.

"After I put this away, let's go out for some lunch. We could go hit up the farmer's market while we're out," Ryan said. "I've had to reschedule again and won't leave for another couple of days."

"I'd like to have some of those fresh spices. Let's do it." She hurried to get the picture out of her sight. After all, she had to protect her emotional health.

Chapter 11

Christopher shuffled into the house. He took off his jacket and threw it over the kitchen chair. He had a killer headache. All of this was getting out of control. He missed Amanda's spark now that she was gone from his office, even while he was furious at her for trying to sue him. For all he knew she'd accuse him of rape, which he would never do. He'd never forced himself on anyone.

Opening the medicine cabinet, he looked over what was in there. Pushing aside the bottles of green Nyquil, he grabbed the Tylenol. Why were there four bottles of Nyquil? And there—two packages of Nyquil capsules too. Why would Skylar have that much Nyquil? She was never sick.

He hadn't spent much time thinking about what his wife was up to while he was getting his kicks. He knew she went out to the bar with Madison from time to time, but other than that, what was she doing? Where was she now? Her mother had always wanted to go to the Virgin Islands but had never gone, and he thought that's why Skylar had decided to go there, of all places. But where was she now? How would he find her?

He picked up his phone and searched for Madison's number. Without thinking, he pushed the green button to make a call to her. Maybe she knew something.

They small-talked for about ten minutes, and he could hear the desire in Madison's voice, but he was consumed at the moment by his need to know.

"Hey, do you know whether Skylar has been seeing anyone?" he asked.

"Well, even if I did, I shouldn't be telling you her secrets, Christopher. You haven't exactly been deserving to know anything about what your wife is doing."

She said this without condemnation, and he could feel her openness to him. Even after all these years, she still had it for him. He grinned, then quickly frowned. "What about the Nyquil? Do you know anything about that?"

"You really need to talk to her about it, but as you probably know, when she realized she couldn't handle alcohol, she began to abuse Nyquil. You know about her naked taxi ride and the guy who took her in, right?"

He had no idea what she was talking about. Madison filled him in on Skylar's alcohol binges and about the last time she was plastered. She said that those prone to substance abuse usually had to go through several different forms of abuse before they realized they needed help to shake their addictions. This was a new side to his wife that he'd not seen before. She'd hidden it.

"I had no idea she had an addiction. How bad is it? Can you really get high with cold syrup?" Christopher asked as he reached for another cookie.

"You sure can. You can get addicted to the dextromethorphan in cough medicine and even suffer from withdrawals. Some people have to go into a rehab center to detox. And I'm sorry to say, but you can probably blame yourself for whatever she's doing. But I'm not criticizing."

"I really need to talk to her. Do you have any idea where she's staying?" he asked.

"No, I don't. Why don't you just call her and tell her you want to talk? Or maybe you can track her phone, but you guys probably don't have 'find my phone' set up."

Did they? He'd have to check.

"Thanks anyway, Madison. Hey, are you busy this weekend? Would you like to get together later? I've been pretty lonely, and I thought you might be too."

"Sure. I work until six though."

"I'll text you later. Thanks for your help."

He grabbed a soda and sat at the table with the bottle of Tylenol and his phone. Searching for Nyquil abuse, he found that Madison was right, and as it settled into his bones that his wife could be harming herself, he began to wonder what else she'd been doing. Life had soured. He swallowed a couple of pills and then checked the location app where he immediately saw a dot blinking. She hadn't turned it off. All this time he could have been checking on her whereabouts. He grabbed his jacket and headed out. Once in his car, he followed the blinking dot to her location. Parking in front of a row of condos, he watched, trying to determine which one she was in.

Twenty minutes later, a Dodge Charger parallel parked a few spaces in front of him and a tall figure got out. He carried a large square bag under his arm. The dreads and the slightly hunched posture gave the man away. It was Ryan Middleton, the same guy Detective Shannon Short had used to bring Christopher in where they'd had their final showdown in Skylar's office. Was this guy Ryan in law enforcement? Nah. At the time, he hadn't known where the detective had gotten the man, but Detective Short had used Ryan for her own purposes when she found out she was pregnant with Christopher's baby. The man had a lot to answer for.

What was the guy carrying in the bag? Was Skylar living with him? Were they—

A stab of something unfamiliar entered his heart.

Who could he talk to about this? Maybe the detective, Tommy Little. Shannon had spoken of him with high regard.

After a brief wait, Ryan entered the condo. Why didn't he just use his key and let himself in? Maybe this wasn't his place. Maybe Skylar rented it and had invited him over. Or maybe she coincidentally lived next door to him and they didn't know each other, but the likelihood of that was not big. He wouldn't do anything without talking to Detective Little, but his face flushed, and he didn't like the feeling of jealousy that coursed through him at the thought of her with another man.

***

The detective was anything but little. Standing as tall as Christopher, he was solid and well-muscled. They measured each other up as men do and the detective welcomed him into his office.

"I suppose you've come about the case."

"Indeed I have. I've got questions that I hope you can answer."

"We've all been affected by this case. I lost a friend and a good detective. Although I've been promoted to her position, I'm working hard on this case. What can I do for you?"

"It's my wife. I'm worried she might be in danger. She may have taken up with a suspect in the case. His first name is Ryan. Detective Short used him there at the end to bring me in to the gathering where she took her life."

"Yes. I've heard about you. You're the guy who can't keep his dick in his pants." He sucked in a big breath, expanding his chest in a subtle show of male dominance that wasn't lost on Christopher. He took a sudden dislike to the man, even while realizing the detective had a right to hold a grudge against him because of Shannon and her pregnancy.

After a moment Detective Little motioned him to sit. "You want a soda?"

"Sure. Got any Dr. Pepper?"

He nodded and left the room, returning shortly with a couple of cold wet cans.

They popped the tops and took swigs. Detective Little leaned back in his chair, arms behind his head. "So, why don't you tell me what has happened between you and Skylar since Shannon's death."

"As far as I know, she took a trip by herself to St. Thomas to get away. She came back the day before the funeral of the latest victim, who was my cousin, in case you weren't aware."

"Oh, believe me, we're aware. This case is top priority. This killing has to stop." The look in his eyes convinced Christopher that Detective Little meant business. The tone of the detective's voice and his rigid body language also communicated the man's disgust of him.

"The condo where Ryan Middleton is staying is owned by a man we have not been able to locate and question—yet. Detective Short mistakenly thought Ryan Middleton was the murderer, using aliases, but we have ruled him out, having no evidence. His landlord is another story. He is using an alias. He has used many aliases, one of which was Steven Quale. We don't know which he's using now. I can almost guarantee your wife is not in danger from Mr. Middleton. But she might be in danger from the killer, if indeed he is the one who owns the condo. She'd be better off out of there."

"Shouldn't you be going and telling her so?"

He scratched his bald head. "We sent an officer over who spoke to Ryan who says he's been barring the door, and we have patrols out frequenting their location. Now if you want to convince your wife to come home, do it. But good luck." Little's facial expression lacked confidence in Christopher's ability to bring that about.

Christopher bristled, even while acknowledging to himself that the man was right. Now he knew she was with this Ryan. He'd be lucky to get her home, and it was his fault.

He stood abruptly, lifting his can in a touché motion, toasting the detective for his skillfulness in calling out his character defects. Detective Little exuded confidence and a high level of competence as well. If anyone could find the killer, it would be him. The intelligence shone from behind his eyes. Heck, he could probably get anyone to believe anything. He himself had already been put in his place for what he really was, and it wasn't pretty. Shame engulfed him.

"I'll be going now," he said. "Thank you."

"My pleasure. We are going to find this guy and put him in a box."

Chapter 12

Madison Wilcox moved her martini glass out of the way to make room for the next one. She caught the young bartender's eye and he nodded. When he brought her refill, he handed her his card. "I circled my number. I spoke to your friend weeks ago and she never got me your name. If you'd ever like to go out, send me a text. I need to get out of this place once in a while." He smiled, though his eyes seemed to have pain behind them, she noticed. She had a thing for wounded men, and he was definitely that. She'd found that most men were, deep inside.

Madison smiled back. She loved male attention, she had to admit, and the awkward guys were the best. Every now and then she had a twinge of guilt, but she preferred to not examine her deeper motives, mostly because they were painful and ugly. Better to keep them hidden. She examined the card. Nathaniel Walker.

She got out her mirror and inspected her lipstick, making sure there were no smudges of red on her pearly whites. Life had gotten boring. Ilene was gone, Skylar was unavailable, Christopher seemed to be having a change of heart, and she had no other friends. She watched Nathaniel move around behind the bar, his muscles flexing through his tight pants. He turned quickly and caught her eye, grinning slightly. *Why not*? She held the card up to him and nodded, then stuffed it into her bag.

She let the last drops of her third martini drip onto her tongue, then she texted Christopher. *Want to ease a girl's loneliness?*

Christopher texted back. *See you in thirty minutes.*

***

What was he doing? This was dangerous. He was just lonely and could use a friend, and she was available. He'd keep his dick in his pants and it would be okay.

Madison let him in the front door of her little duplex. She crooked her finger for him to come and grabbed a small cooler. He followed her, curious, as she weaved through the house and out the back door. His gaze remained on her as she moved across the backyard and then through a wooden garden gate to the walking path that led straight into the hardwood forest. After a short, silent three-minute walk, she veered off to the left and came upon a small secluded clearing. Someone had built a little cabin entirely out of recycled windows, of all different shapes, sizes, and colors. When she reached the door, she turned to him.

"I often come here to have a place to be out in nature. I can hear the birds, the wind and rain, and the breeze comes in through the screens on both sides. It makes me feel alive. I sometimes sleep out here too."

He nodded. "Who put this here?"

She opened the door and smiled.

"You built it?" he asked, amazed.

She threw her dark brown hair over her shoulder, her full lips curving up in a shy grin, a look he'd never seen on her before. Her exotic beauty was what drew men to her. Hopefully she knew how to be careful. Her looks could get her into trouble.

"I built this from a bunch of windows I picked up at a donation center. The rest is built out of wood planks from an old barn. I rented a truck and filled it full. All together I built this place for only five hundred dollars."

"That's impressive. I bet you like coming out here to recharge." He followed her into the single room, about the size of a two-car garage. She'd fixed it up like a little studio apartment, complete with a composting toilet and a washbasin on a little table, with a large pitcher of water next to it that she filled from a hand pump well outside the side door of the little building. She'd done a decent job. Better than he could have done, he had to admit.

"I have this propane cooking stove in here. It's all I need, since I don't spend a lot of time here. It's comfortable about half the year. My next project is to see how I can insulate it for better temperature control."

She motioned to the only piece of furniture, a short sofa covered with a denim quilt, then fixed them both a cup of tea and sat next to him.

"So, what do you do when you come out here?"

She motioned to the bookcase standing off in the shadows. "Read."

"That's it?"

She nodded, at a loss for words. Her fun-loving posture was gone. Maybe she had a deeper side that he'd never seen. For some strange reason, this made him desire her less and respect her more.

They talked until it was too dark to see, having had only one interruption, when Lisa tried to call him. The woman wouldn't leave him alone. He needed to deal with that situation, because it wasn't going to go away.

He had picked up on Madison's signals that she'd be open to physical contact, but he couldn't do it. Not this time. Not after the detective had cut him down to size and caused him to lose his self-respect, which he wasn't at all convinced he could get back.

By the time he was ready to leave, she had accepted that he was turning her down. She told him to give her a call the next day if he wanted to talk. She had a date with the bartender, she said, but would be in no later than ten o'clock. She never stayed out late the first date with a new guy. He nodded, then gave her a quick hug. He left and drove home, his thoughts anything but settled.

Now that he'd found Skylar and seen the guy she was with, his jealousy was aroused and he realized he wasn't ready to lose her. She had always treated him well, and he had disrespected her and her commitment to their marriage. Why had he assumed she'd want him back? Looked like she was well on her way to leaving him for good. He flung his jacket into the passenger seat and swore. He didn't have a clue how he was going to pay for everything. Hopefully the attorney would help in the case of Lisa and Claire. That kind of money was going to be hard to come by. All alone now, the harsh reality of his indiscretions landed on him like a boulder, and he was pinned under it.

Chapter 13

The phone buzzed on his nightstand and Christopher cracked an eye open. A number appeared, in his area code. Only a hint of daylight left in this day, from the looks of it. He grabbed it, punched the button, and said hello.

"Christopher? It's Lisa."

Her voice was sharp and loud. He grimaced, then rubbed his face. "Lisa." This situation with the woman he'd had a one-night stand with, who'd not had the sense to do anything to prevent pregnancy, just might be the worst of his problems. She wanted half a million from him to drop the court case she'd filed against him after learning the results of the paternity test, and it seemed there was nothing he could do. Should he fight it? He needed to consult his own attorney. Why had he answered? Her tone was mean and condescending. But maybe that's what he deserved. The hole he'd dug was getting deeper.

"What are you calling for?" he said.

"You've had time to think, so now you need to tell me what you're going to do about this. My husband died six months ago."

He didn't want to have this conversation.

"I have an appointment with my attorney in a couple of weeks and then I'll let you know. You really can't get away with blaming me." It wasn't his fault. Was it? His anger rose and he jumped from the bed. He paced the floor as he listened to her whine.

"You have no idea what this has done to my life, Christopher. Like a fool I believed you were a decent guy, but you dropped me like a rock when the next pretty face came along. You bear equal responsibility. Man-up and face it."

She was trying to trap him. Finally, he said, "How old is she now?"

"Ten and a half."

Suddenly it occurred to him that he might like to meet his only child.

"I'd like to meet her."

"Absolutely not. You done your damage and you don't need to be doin' any more."

"I am not paying anything without being able to see my daughter."

She was quiet for a moment, then she said, "I'm not heartless, Christopher. Why don't you meet us after school tomorrow? I'll introduce you but do *not* tell her you're her father. I'm not ready for that. After school. Three-thirty. We'll walk to the soda fountain around the corner. You can buy her a root beer float, her favorite. Then it's looking like the courts will decide where we go from there." She hung up abruptly.

Christopher grabbed his wallet off the dresser and threw it against the wall, where it burst open and a shower of cards sprayed out.

He bent down to pick them up. The last one lay face up. He'd found it at the coffee shop a month ago when things soured with Amanda. Now that office slut was suing him. Lisa was suing him too. His wife was with another man and his finances were going to be in disarray for a long time to come, it appeared.

"The Bradshaws," the card said. Pastor Lamont Bradshaw and his wife, life coach Erica Bradshaw. He lay the card down next to the ever-growing stack of bills. Skylar always took care of those things. He dropped down on the chair, sorting through the stack, then he grabbed his phone. Maybe he was acting impulsively, but so be it. He dialed Skylar's number.

"Hello, Christopher," her smooth voice said.

"What'cha doin', sweetie. Give me a kiss," came a different voice from the background.

"Who was that?" Christopher said.

"Oh. Wasn't me. It was the parrot. Coco."

"Where are you, anyway?" he asked.

"Not your business. So, why are you calling?"

"Well..." he paused, unsure whether to risk asking. He didn't much like the feeling of needing the person he'd cheated on.

"Come on, out with it. You must have had a reason to call."

"I—"

"Can't be that hard, can it?"

"I want to be honest with you, Skylar. I have a favor to ask. I know I don't deserve it, but it would be really nice if you would come with me tomorrow. You remember that woman Lisa who called wanting money for her child she claimed I fathered? She's after me again, and I insisted on seeing the girl. I'm in a buttload of trouble with this, but Lisa agreed to let me meet Claire, and I would really like it if you'd come with me tomorrow afternoon. Would you?"

"I don't know what help I'd be."

"You'll get what's coming to you, *brother,*" the very human-sounding voice said.

"Was that the bird again? What's he saying that for? Sounds like a threat. Did he hear it somewhere?"

"I don't know. One night I came home and he whispered it. I thought someone was in the condo with me. It freaked me out, let me tell you."

"Why don't you think about coming home? It might be safer than where you are."

"Where do you think I am, Christopher?"

Busted. "Um, well, I realized I could probably track you by your phone's location app, and sure enough, it was still turned on. I drove to the vicinity and found where you are. Are you living alone?"

"No, I live with a parrot." She gave a short laugh. "I'm not interested in giving you that information. How long have you been spying on me?"

"I only thought of it a few days ago. I'm worried about your safety, Sky. Please consider moving back home, at least until all this business is over with the killer."

"I don't know why you care, and I am *not* going to move back in with you. But I will consider going with you tomorrow for moral support, but not as a couple. Got that?"

"I guess that's as good as I could expect. I deserve worse."

"Yes, you do. Now I've got to go. Text me with the details. See you then."

After she hung up on him, he rubbed his thick curly hair. He might be able to reverse the downhill course of his life, but it wasn't going to be easy.

Chapter 14

The next evening Madison Wilcox sat at the bar and flipped her silky brown hair over her shoulder, then looked behind her for Nathaniel. She enjoyed the V, a nice bar on the edge of DC, preferring it over the Martini where she'd met Nathaniel and where she used to go with Skylar. Nathaniel had said to meet him here at six, and he was fifteen minutes late.

She checked her lipstick and declined a second drink. If he didn't show soon, she wouldn't wait. She was getting tired of the dating scene. Maybe she should just take a break.

The older gentleman sitting two seats down gave her a sympathetic smile. "Hey, pretty lady, I'd take you home with me if the wife weren't home."

"That won't be necessary," a voice said behind her. She swiveled and there he was, his normally spiky blond hair in disarray, matted down in a few spots.

"Nathaniel. I thought you stood me up."

"Sorry. I had a phone call I couldn't get free of." The music came on, modern rap with a strange beat. She frowned and he said, "How about we go somewhere else with a bigger dance floor? I know how much you like to dance. Plus, there's some wait staff that migrated from the Martini who rub me the wrong way."

One of the waiters approached with a carry-out box. "The chef asked me to give this to Ms. Madison," he said, smiling.

"For me?" Madison said.

"On the house. Rob saw you come in and he started this for you right away, since you always order it. He knows it's your favorite. And I could see you are leaving, so I put it in a carryout box with a plastic fork for you."

"Well, that is sweet. Please let him know how much I appreciate it." She turned to Nathaniel. "Do you mind sitting here a few minutes? I'll share."

The waiter nodded and Nathaniel sat down, picking up a fork. "You first," he said.

He smiled charmingly, and she returned the smile.

The warm gooey cake sat atop a mound of cold vanilla bean ice cream and she watched as the hot fudge ran like lava down over the frozen scoop. She bit into it and sighed. After a few minutes of culinary bliss, she realized Nathaniel had stopped eating.

"What's wrong?" she said.

He shook his head slightly, then spoke quietly. "Those people I mentioned? They're here. I'd just rather not have to talk to them."

"Okay, I'll hurry." She took a few more bites and they left.

"I'm sorry to rush you out. I didn't think about the possibility of seeing them when we planned to meet here. But this other place will be better anyway."

His car was clean inside, as well-groomed as he always was, although tonight Madison sensed something was off. As he drove away from the curb, he seemed unusually watchful and his eyes darted around. When his phone rang, he nearly jumped out of his jacket. He glanced at the screen and began to slow down.

"I'm sorry, but I have to take this call." He pulled into a body shop parking lot and got out, walking to the back of the car. She rolled down her window to get some fresh air, then bent down to run her finger along the edge of her new heels. The side was cutting in just below her ankle bone.

"Skylar?" Nathaniel's voice resonated from the back of the car. She froze, listening, her head still down. A chill traveled the length of her spine. "What do you want me to do?" Nathaniel continued. She raised up slowly and turned to look, but he was facing away from the car now and all she could hear was his muffled voice.

Night had fallen. Something was wrong. Should she get out? They were on the edge of town, with no one around. She scanned the car for something to use to defend herself, then felt through her purse, while the muffled voice continued. She could see nothing. She opened the glove box and shoved her hand under the maps and manuals. Her fingers curled around a small item. A little bag of miniature tools. She shut the glovebox and shoved the toolkit in the pocket of her sweater just as the car door opened and Nathaniel slid in.

"Sorry to make you wait. That was my boss. He doesn't want to work with me on the schedule, and I really need some days off in a row next month."

Madison turned away and bit her lip, but not one to shy away from confrontation, she said, "What does that have to do with Skylar? What interest does your boss have in her?" She watched his response closely, challenging him with her eyes as well as her words.

He coughed, then looked back, holding her gaze steadily. "You're not going to make things easy for me, are you."

"Nope. Take me back now. I want nothing to do with you."

Nathaniel sat with the car running, looking straight ahead. Then he said, "No. I can't do that. I'm going to have to hold you for a while. You'll just have to deal with that. Let me have your purse and your phone." He reached over to his door and pushed a button. The child-lock. Crap. Did he have a weapon?

"Forget it, Nathaniel. Take me back." She pulled her phone out of her purse and held down the button, trying to get to the screen where she could call 9-1-1. He grabbed for it.

The phone flew out of her hand and across the back of the seat. When she turned to look for it, he snatched her purse and tossed it back to join the phone. Now both were out of her reach. Then he pulled a wicked-looking knife from his pocket. He had quick reflexes.

"Are you really doing this?" she said.

"Turn around and put your hands behind your back or I'll slit your throat."

She glared, then decided cooperation was the best way to prevent her own death. "You're never going to get away with this or whatever else you have planned, you know. This county is crawling with law enforcement related to this serial killer case. If you let me go, I'll never breathe a word."

"There are better ways to make sure you don't breathe a word," Nathaniel said. He held the tip of the blade against the back of her neck, then came the sound of duct tape ripping off a spool and she felt him wrap the sticky tape around her wrists.

"Where do you plan to take me? Are you going to kill me? If you're the killer, which there's every indication you are now that I think about it, you might as well get it over with."

The seatbelt alarm dinged as he began to drive. "Shit. Put your seatbelt on, would you?"

The windows had fogged up and she couldn't see out. Since she was tied up, he had to pull over and come around and do it himself. Served him right. Then he adjusted the fan settings to defog the windshield and pulled out into the road again, leaving civilization behind. What kind of trouble had she gotten herself into?

He pulled over again. "I should blindfold you. Wish I had a gag too." He got out of the car again and opened the trunk. When he came back, he was carrying an old knitted stocking cap, frayed and filthy. "Bend forward so I can put this on you."

Shaking now from fear, she had no choice but to comply while he pulled it down over her eyes.

Chapter 15

Skylar loved the relaxed Friday morning routine, the one day they both had free, that included breakfast in bed. She and Ryan would scurry out from under their fluffy comforter to split the breakfast duties. They had made it an art form, each trying to outdo the other. When it came time to plate the food, Ryan supplied the artistic touches, laying green avocado wedges around the scoop of rice and adding bacon. Skylar then lumped scrambled eggs around the outside of the rice volcano. With artistic flair, Ryan pressed a hole in the center of the rice and dribbled ketchup down the side. But this morning something was off.

Ryan said, "I got to be gone for about five days, baby. Do you have anywhere you can go to be safer than here? I don't like you being alone all that time."

"Are you leaving today?"

He nodded, not volunteering anything more.

"I'll be fine. I'm a big girl now, in case you hadn't noticed." She smiled. She liked him being concerned for her, but she also liked being independent.

Ryan frowned. "Can't you go stay with your friend Madison?"

Skylar's back stiffened. She didn't want to talk to Madison. She'd grown leery of her, distrusting her motives, especially after finding out that Madison had moved in on Christopher. "No, I don't want to do that. Not Madison."

"How about going back to your house? It is partly yours, and you'd be safer there than here."

"Why would you say that? Is there something you're not telling me?"

"Of course not."

She tried to make eye contact, but Ryan kept his head down, looking into the remains of his milky coffee.

She leaped from the bed without grace, her robe tangling in the covers. "Are you hiding something? Why won't you tell me what it is, Ryan? Is that too much to ask, after all this time together?"

He shook his head. "I can't."

"Well, okay then. I can't stay with you if you're hiding things from me."

She walked quickly into the kitchen with plates and mugs, her heart hurting from his apparent lack of trust, then she gathered the laundry and threw it into the machine. She'd pack and get out, if that's what he wanted. He'd told her nothing about where he was going, and he wouldn't tell her why he was so nervous. Things were not adding up, and she didn't like it.

She followed Ryan into his bedroom. "You're hiding something from me. If it has anything to do with me, you need to tell me, Ryan." He folded a shirt and began filling his carryon bag with clothes.

"Could you feed Coco while I'm gone? I'm sorry I can't tell you more. You'll just have to accept it for now and trust me. I care about you, and that's one reason I can't tell you."

She crossed her arms. "I don't buy that, Ryan."

"That's because you don't know."

"And you won't tell me. Great. I see how little you trust me."

Ryan pressed his lips together tightly, and she could see she'd get no more from him. Now he was upset because she wouldn't trust him. When he left, she didn't bother to go downstairs or give him a hug or kiss. Served him right. After pacing the floor for a few minutes, she pulled out her phone and texted him that she'd check on Coco. At least the bird liked her.

She'd get ready for her time with Christopher and then she wasn't sure what she'd do after they were done. She didn't have to listen to Ryan, did she? Maybe she'd just stay here in the condo anyway. With the door barred, Coco as watch bird, and her new pepper spray, she should be good. She might not get much sleep, but she could handle it. If it didn't go well, she might see about going back home to her own bedroom.

Chapter 16

Christopher picked up the card on the counter. He'd left it out, thinking he might call to see if Pastor Lamont did any counseling. He looked them up online and liked what he saw. The pastor had warm eyes that crinkled in the corners and a friendly smile, one that looked like it could pierce the darkness inside and still like you afterward. He called the number and spoke with his wife, who gave him a canceled appointment for the next morning. He could go before work. Thank goodness. He'd had too many days off lately trying to take care of everything after Skylar left. He couldn't let himself get fired, especially now.

Skylar pulled into the driveway and honked.

Christopher folded his body into the compact car they jointly owned, and she looked to him for directions. Eye contact was difficult with so much unresolved between them. He had hurt Skylar, and she was hurting him in return. But no one could fault her for it.

They parked next to the school playground and got out of the car. Christopher searched for a face he could barely remember. When Lisa detached from the crowd, he watched her approach with a girl who was nearing puberty.

"Hi, Lisa," he said. "This is my wife Skylar."

"Nice to meet you," Lisa said. She held out her hand and Skylar shook it politely. "And this is Claire."

They all looked at the girl, and Skylar bent down to her level. Claire dropped her eyes and wouldn't make eye contact, so Skylar stepped back.

"Claire, this is Mr. Phillips," Lisa said. Christopher held out his hand to the girl. She looked at him and slowly placed her hand in his and he covered it with his other.

"You're my dad?" she said.

He looked at Lisa, who shrugged. "I had to tell her something."

"Yes, it appears that I am. I'm looking forward to getting to know you. Let's go get ice cream. Your mother tells me there is a good place just down the street."

She smiled at him and slipped her small hand in his, then turned and gave Skylar a gloating look.

Skylar reared back and Lisa shrugged, apologetic.

Christopher and Claire led the way, and Skylar hung back with Lisa.

"I'm sorry about that, Skylar," Lisa said. "I'm not sure why she reacted that way to you, but she seems kind of jealous that you're with her father. She also misses my husband, who has only been gone for about six months. We're both still grieving, and her young mind is a little confused."

"It takes about a year to get over the worst of it. I've seen a lot of grief in my counseling business."

Claire kept turning around and making faces at Skylar, and at one point, Lisa pulled her aside and spoke to her about it, after which she behaved more respectfully.

When they finished their ice cream, they walked back to the parking lot and said their goodbyes. Lisa promised to call to discuss matters further.

On the trip home, Christopher told her about all the hot water he'd gotten himself into. "I've made an appointment tomorrow morning to meet with Pastor Lamont Bradshaw for some counseling. You might want to come with me sometime."

"Now why would I want to come to your counseling sessions, Christopher? I got nothin' to say to anyone. And if I did, I wouldn't pick the same counselor you're going to see."

He shook his head. "Okay, I get it." He was silent for a few minutes. Then, before he could stop himself, he asked her again if she'd like to move back in. She shook her head.

"No, I don't think so. I'm not ready for that. I like it where I am for now."

"Are you...with someone?"

Skylar didn't answer for a few long seconds. "It really doesn't matter at this point, does it?"

"It matters to me, Sky."

She looked at him as if to assess his truthfulness, and then, satisfied, she turned away. It would take some work for him to warm her back up, he could see that now. She would not be susceptible to his charm, he knew that, so he didn't even try.

"I would like it if you came home, but if you're not ready, it's okay."

"I'm not."

She pulled into their driveway, the large evergreen scratching against the car. Christopher coughed. More evidence of her clumsiness, but today she hardly cared. She waited for him to get out.

"Take care of yourself and be careful," he said. "It's not safe out there with the killer at large."

"I know. I've taken precautions. Talk to you sometime."

She sped off while he wiped his eye. What had he expected? That she'd still love him enough to forgive him instantly for all his cheating? That she'd be sympathetic to his problems? He deserved her reluctance and much worse than that. It had been a stressful afternoon for him. All he could do now was wait and try to handle his own business in the healthiest way possible.

Chapter 17

Skylar arrived back at the condo and parked in her usual spot. When she entered the house, Coco greeted her with a "Hi, cutie. Give me a kiss." She opened the cage and let him out, turned on the hot water pot for a cup of tea, and slipped upstairs to put on some leggings and a large cable-knit sweater and her slippers. She jumped when Coco turned on his music. Ryan had trained the bird to talk to Alexa. He liked jazz, so that's what he always asked for. "Alexa, give me some jazz," he'd say. Cute, but annoying, like a child who wants to sing the same song on repeat at bedtime. Not that she'd know about that. She was thirty-four years old and had no children, unlike her cheating husband. Didn't he know how to buy a condom? It wasn't that hard. She shook her head, trying not to feel sorry for him or herself, but it was getting harder by the day.

Her phone vibrated on the counter. Vesta.

"Hello, chile, how you doing?" The woman's warm voice soothed her unease.

"I'm fine."

"Are you alone? I don't think I'd want to be alone with the killer still out there. I wish we'd get a break in this case, but so far, we got nothing. The killer is either very experienced, very smart, has a good helper, or is able to keep things from the investigation somehow. This one's a bitch."

Skylar chipped at her nail polish. "I'm taking precautions. I will go bar the door as soon as we get off the phone."

"Make sure you do. And keep your phone charged and have it with you at all times. You hear me, chile?"

"It will stay in my pocket at all times."

"Okay. You call me if you need to for any reason. Even during the night."

"Will do, Vesta. Don't worry about me."

"You still haven't told me if you have anyone with you. But I'll respect your privacy."

"If I felt like I could, I would. But get this. It seems Christopher is wanting to change his ways."

"That's great! Isn't it?"

"Well, yes, for him it is. Needs to happen. But it's not easy for me. There comes a point at which a person can't go back because they've moved on. I don't know how I feel about ever going back to him."

"I understand, chile. I'll let you get back to what you were doing. Check in with me, even just a text, to let me know you're okay. Deal?"

Skylar agreed and ended the call. She put Alexa back in the cabinet without unplugging the device, wondering whether Coco carried on conversations with the virtual assistant while they were gone. Then she carried her tea to the living room to sit in the comfy chair.

She wanted to look at the picture of herself and Christopher again. Maybe it was time to try to sort it out and make some decisions for herself. She scuffed to the back door. "Be right back," she said to the bird.

"Aye aye, Captain," he said. She smiled. He was one smart bird.

Night had fallen, and no one was around on the back side of the complex. She pulled her key out of her pocket where she'd placed it. After retrieving the picture in its frame, she hurried back inside. The music was back on. How did that happen? Pushing the door shut with her foot, she entered the kitchen and realized the bird had opened the cupboard and pulled Alexa out and was pecking at the round disc, swaying and bobbing his head and muttering, "Don't worry, be happy."

"Give it up, Coco," she said. She sat back in her chair and gazed at the two young people in the picture who looked as if they were quite happy together. That did not compute, so she rose and retrieved the brace for the front door and installed it. After reading for a while, she put the bird in his cage and covered it, then went upstairs. Pulling the covers down, she noticed that Ryan had made her bed with the sheet set Nathaniel had left for him back on the island. Sweet of him.

She lay down on the cool sheets, then realized she'd left her phone downstairs. Crap. Too drowsy to go get it, she picked up the paperback book she'd brought upstairs with her from the floor next to the bed, then realized the horror story might not be such a good idea under the circumstances, so she closed her eyes and tried to puzzle out her situation.

She awoke and looked at the clock. Midnight. A twinge of fear ran up her back and she shivered, pulling the covers up under her chin, but she lay and listened and heard nothing, so she went downstairs. Coco was silent. Retrieving a glass from the dishwasher, she filled it with ice and then water. Wide awake now, she decided to clean out her purse. Dumping everything out, she sorted things by category. Down at the bottom was a plastic tube. Did it have anything in it? She popped the lid open and turned it over in her hand. A half-smoked joint slid into her palm, left over from the island. Somehow it had made it through airport security.

Smoking had helped her anxiety before, so maybe this was a good idea. And tonight she had plenty of anxiety. She lit up over the stove and let the smoke go up the exhaust fan. Thirty minutes later she was feeling pretty chill, so she headed back to bed. She lay down on the rosebud-printed sheets, smiling at all the ways Ryan showed he cared, then she connected her ear buds to her phone and opened her playlist. Honestly, she really liked Ryan. He calmed her and was so easy to live with. This latest deceptiveness disturbed her because it wasn't like him. But music was exquisite while stoned, so she listened and let herself drift into dreamland without a care in the world. Just how she liked it.

Chapter 18

After a bumpy end to the quiet ride, Nathaniel removed the stocking cap so Madison could see. They had taken a rough gravel road into some trees, and he motioned with the flashlight in one hand and the knife in the other for her to get out. Madison followed him a short distance through the thick trees until they came to a small hut, even smaller than her little window house.

"I'm sorry Madison, but I'm going to have to leave you here. I know it's not the most comfortable place, but at least you'll have water. Someone will be back. Either me or the boss. I'll leave a light on so you can see."

"You bastard." The room was small, with lots of wood paneling inside. A window had been placed on one side and another in the back, but the cabin was rustic, with no plumbing. An electric lamp and a space heater were signs it had power from some source, but it seemed very remote, causing her fear to escalate.

"You don't understand. It isn't my fault," Nathaniel said.

"Everyone has a choice. If you make the wrong one, then it *is* your fault." What could she say to find out more about what was going on? She jerked on the rope by which she was now tied. A couple of screw eyes had already been twisted into the wall next to an old mattress. Could this place have been used for this kind of purpose before? Nathaniel tied one of her feet to the bolt with a piece of rope, then cut the tape off her wrists with his knife and tied one wrist to the other bolt.

"Are you planning to rape me? Kill me? Or just keep me out of the way so you can do it to someone else? Whatever it is, let's talk about it and figure out a better way. I don't think you want to do whatever it is." She'd gone with her gut. His eyes were haunted, and his actions lacked determination. But she could be wrong. "You can talk to me," she said.

He moved around the room, getting her set so she would not be dead before someone found her. "You aren't getting anything out of me, so stop trying."

"Can I relieve myself before you go? Assuming you are going."

"Fine. There's an outhouse out back. But don't get any ideas about trying to run. You'll only get hurt." He untied her from the bolts and pointed with the knife toward the back of the hut, walking close behind her and shining the flashlight ahead of her.

Inside the outhouse, which contained no toilet paper, the little toolkit from the glovebox fell out of her pocket onto the floor. She'd forgotten about it. Nathaniel would've found it if he'd searched her, but either he was too shaken up or he was only carrying out orders, coerced by someone else. If she had to bet on it, she doubted he was a killer. But maybe his nerves indicated excitement about what he was going to do. Or it could be anxiety about carrying it out.

She felt around in the dark and finally found the kit, then she tucked the kit into her panties instead of her pocket and emerged from the rickety outhouse.

When she looked at Nathaniel, she had a sudden flashback of playing villains and secret agents with her three brothers outside. They formed teams and used walkie-talkies to communicate with their own teammate. The only difference here was that Nathaniel had a knife and it was dark. She sized him up, and just as she had evaded and dodged her brothers, she darted past Nathaniel and took off across the stubbly ground, not able to see where she was going, but hopeful she'd be able to find a place to hide.

He cursed and took off after her. When she was almost to the dirt road, she failed to see the hole and in went her right foot. With a horrid thud she landed face down in the dirt, the air knocked out of her and searing pain in her lower leg.

He was on her instantly, nearly running past her. As she struggled to draw a breath, he struggled to catch his. A terrible scream erupted from her mouth.

"Help me!" she screamed before everything went black.

Chapter 19

Vesta sat at her desk in the office she shared with Detective Little. She'd finally finished organizing her files, a detested chore, but when completed it made her life so much more pleasant. Tommy had been fun to be around lately too. He was still chatting it up with someone in an office across the hall. She'd watched his muscles flex beneath his uniform shirt, then caught his eye when she went for a cup of hot tea. He winked. She blushed. And then he asked if she'd like to go out for a bite to eat after she finished. It was going to be a good night. She could feel it. She deserved a little fun in her life, though she seldom let down her guard enough. Every time she let a man get close it turned out poorly, but she'd known Tommy for several years now. Maybe this time would be different.

The excitement had been building, and they both knew it was against department policy to get involved, but attraction and need often ignore rules.

After a nice dinner during which he'd flirted outrageously, he invited her to his townhouse. He'd touched her several times already, and as they walked the short distance from the car, he captured her hand in his.

Tommy's place was meticulously clean and tidy for someone who lived alone. They'd found a TV series they were both into, and the new season had just come available, so they sat together on the soft leather sofa. She curled her legs up and he reached over and put his arm around her, allowing her to scoot close. She lay her head on the front of his shoulder. Oooh, nice. It had been too long.

After the first episode she turned to him, and he leaned forward and took her lips with his. Pent-up hunger gripped her, and she responded in kind. Almost before she could blink, he had her sweater off and his hands on her bra hooks.

"We shouldn't be doing this." Her breathy voice sounded unconvincing, even to her.

"Oh baby, you have been driving me crazy for months. You are so beautiful."

Just as his hands were going where no hands had gone in a long time, a loud rattling sounded on the coffee table.

"Shit." He disrupted their flow and looked at the caller ID and said, "I'm sorry, baby. I have to take this."

She had never seen him with his shirt off. A line of chest hair led down his torso and into the top of his still-buttoned khakis. Then she caught a word that made her overheated blood freeze.

"Madison Wilcox, you say? Missing?" He walked to the window, looking out into the night. "Yeah, okay. I'll be in shortly."

She'd seen his masked look before, which usually preceded bad news he didn't want to know about. The guy was quite sensitive, underneath the cold persona he usually showed to strangers.

"I'm sorry, Vesta. I have to go in."

"I'll come with you."

"I know you want to be supportive, but I'll take care of this. No need for both of us to have our evenings disrupted."

"They already are, so there's no difference."

"I hear what you're saying, but this doesn't require both of us. I'll take you home. You should get some sleep. I'll call you later and tell you what I found out."

He wasn't going to budge, so she agreed and went to use the bathroom. He could get a bit stubborn at times.

His bathroom was as clean as everything else. Her kind of guy. Was his medicine cabinet as neat inside as everything was outside? Her detective mind chewed on the transgression a moment. It wouldn't hurt, would it? She opened it carefully so it wouldn't make any noise.

Just as she suspected, the cabinet was as organized and tidy as everything else. Except for one thing.

Tucked away on the narrow top shelf were two bags. One was the evidence bag from the crime scene with a smooth white pill inside, and the other was a separate bag with a bigger number of the same pill. About twenty, it appeared. Why hadn't he turned in the one she'd found? Maybe he'd decided it wasn't important and he could just add it to his own collection. But it was a pill for ED. Why would such a virile-appearing man need something for erectile dysfunction?

When she came out of the bathroom, she kept her face as blank as possible.

He drove her home in silence while she stewed about Tommy not letting her come along. Her mind churned. Something wasn't adding up. Why would the pill be at the scene of the fire that killed Briana? They could belong to Briana's husband, but he was ten years younger than Detective Little. Even less likely he'd need them.

By the time they reached her home, she was sure she wouldn't be able to sleep, so she fixed a cup of chamomile tea to calm her and sat in her rocker. The conflicting thoughts produced enough dissonance that she couldn't settle down until she had some answers. Just what was going on here?

After debating with herself, she made a decision. She rose from the rocker and shoved her arms into her jacket, then left the house, remembering to lock the door at the last minute.

Arriving at the station at 12:30 a.m., she sat in her car in the empty parking lot, not seeing Tommy's car anywhere, and no lights shone from any of the windows. Who had called it in? And what exactly had they called in? That Madison was missing? Maybe it was Skylar who'd discovered it. She'd try her.

No answer.

She called Detective Little.

No answer.

She then tried Madison herself.

Still no answer.

One more call to the FBI agent who was in charge of the local case. He answered, but said he knew nothing about Madison Wilcox or that she'd been reported missing.

Maybe it was Christopher who called it in. She looked up his number and dialed.

Chapter 20

Nathaniel sized up the condo. He knew it inside and out, because he'd lived there for a year before renting it to Ryan. Thinking over his next steps, he wondered about the bird. It could be a problem if it was still alive.

Briana was supposed to be the last victim, but now Skylar had to go. She matched the criteria for a victim in this case, being a cheater, and she knew too much. Ryan would be really angry about this, but it couldn't be helped. He'd find someone else eventually. But would Ryan ever forgive him? He supposed it didn't matter, considering his track record at success in life.

His phone vibrated with an incoming message. His boss. The boss always had to be appeased. And he, Nathaniel, would never be free.

He started the car, drove carefully into the alley, and rolled to a stop, parallel parking in the single spot behind the condo. He grabbed a duffel bag and his flashlight, careful to make no noise with the car door. He didn't want this to happen here in the condo for risk of being overheard, but he really had no other choice. The gag would help. He would have taken Skylar to the hut, but it was occupied now. The demon boss must be appeased if he, Nathaniel, was to ever get any peace. But he swore this would be the last.

After Skylar, he'd take his leave of humanity and never look back. Skylar was the end of the road for him.

He crept to the rear of the condo. A wood fence surrounded a small back patio with a grill. The code to unlock the keypad on the door probably hadn't been changed. When he checked, he found the door cracked with a sock stuck at the bottom to hold it open. The boss must have used the code he'd given him, gone inside, and left it unlocked for him. They wouldn't see each other. He'd been given explicit instructions each time. He was to do the setup, and the boss would finish. If only he'd been smarter as a young person. None of this would have happened. He'd be free and living a decent life somewhere, maybe even with a real, soft, warm woman, instead of bartending and carrying out orders to do unspeakable things to them. No, they weren't completely innocent, but they didn't deserve this. He'd never been told why he'd been given certain tasks, but he'd figured it out. The boss had to be psychotic. It was the only explanation that made any sense.

Nathaniel glanced at his watch. Two o'clock. The condo was silent. Either the bird was sound asleep—or dead—which would be sad. He hadn't meant to hurt the bird the night he visited Ryan.

He silently climbed the stairs inside to the bedrooms, hoping Skylar was snoring so he could be sure she was asleep. He removed his pistol from his back pocket and approached the lump lying in the bed, on the sheets he'd printed and given to Ryan. He was no expert at this kind of stuff, even though he'd done it several other times. The boss had seen an opportunity to use him, and that's why he'd gotten mixed up in this mess in the first place. He, not the boss, would be the one accused and sentenced to death if caught.

As he looked down at Skylar's soft features, he thought about her spunk and determination, and how she embodied the feminine wiles that made women so irresistible, and he just couldn't. He hadn't known the others, but he knew Skylar. Perspiration broke out on his forehead and he nearly peed himself upon the next thought.

He'd help her escape. And if he died trying, well then, it was what he deserved, but at least he'd die doing something good. This new resolve rose in him and became a force of nature in its strength. He would shake off the weight of his past and forge a new beginning. God willing.

Where was the boss? How could he get Skylar out of the condo? As he was hesitating, he heard a soft throat clearing. Oh god, he was in the closet behind him. Waiting for him to prepare the victim. He nudged Skylar with his hand, and bent over her.

"Skylar, wake up," he whispered close to her ear.

"Oooh, baby, you came home!"

"No, no, it's not Ryan. It's Nathaniel."

Her eyes flew open. They were confused. "You're right," she said, a weird smile on her face. She giggled.

Somehow her response, with its lack of fear, gave him courage to do something to save her, and he tried not to grin. God, it felt good, just knowing he was going to stand and fight.

"Nathaniel? The bartender? What are you doing here? I must be dreaming."

"You're not. See the gun? I need you to get out of bed. Now. Quietly."

She sat up, a look of horror on her face. She wasn't acting quite right. He didn't want to use his flashlight. A nightlight on the opposite wall in the shape of a butterfly gave off the only light in the room.

"What's wrong with you? You act like you're stoned."

"I am stoned." She giggled.

"Well, take your stoned self into the bathroom and put this on. Now." He handed her the outfit he'd been told to use this time. It appeared very insubstantial. He'd like to see it on a woman too, if he were honest.

"This little thing? I can't fit into this."

"It says, 'one size fits most.' It's stretchy."

"What're we doing here, Nathaniel? Is this a rape?"

Why did every woman assume he wanted to rape them? "Shut up and do as you're told, bitch," he said in a loud voice. Get in there, strip, and put this on. I'll be right outside the door with the enforcer."

"Okay, okay, don't get testy with me, young man."

He didn't answer. In a few minutes she was out, wearing the one-piece black fishnet with nothing underneath. God, what a beautiful woman. They all were.

"Now, back to the bedroom." He stood in her way and jerked his head down the hall in the opposite direction, holding eye contact with her for a moment. She might be stoned, but she wasn't slow. Adrenaline was a marvelous thing sometimes.

She tiptoed down the hall, the carpet muffling their footsteps. She turned once, and he put his finger to his lips, but before he could give her the signal to be quiet, she blurted out, "Give me a break. I just need a glass of water."

Downstairs, a female voice said, "I'm sorry, I didn't get that."

Another voice, muffled, came from the kitchen. "Alexa, play some jazz."

The music came on. That would cover their sounds of escape.

Nathaniel put his mouth close to her ear. "Quick, out back to the car."

They hurried down the stairs, hearing a thud from upstairs. He hoped the boss had tripped over something in the dark and broken his neck. That would solve all their problems.

"Ouch, ouch, ouch, ouch," Skylar said, dancing over the rocks and sticks in the backyard in her fishnetted feet.

She slid quickly into the front seat of the car. The little Corolla bumped and bounced out of the alley and then Nathaniel floored it.

"I can't believe it," he said. "Yippee! Let me get you out of here. I think we're home free now."

"Where are we going, Nathaniel?" she asked, sounding almost excited to be going on some kind of adventure. He couldn't believe it. He shook his head while she smoothed down her hair, completely oblivious of her immodest outfit. He tried to focus.

"I am taking you to Madison," he said.

"Where is she?" Skylar's perfectly pruned eyebrows rose a notch. They'd be part of her hairline before he finished talking.

"I came across an old hut out in the woods. It's about forty-five minutes from here. The boss has been there once before, but I don't think he will be able to find it again."

She twisted and looked back. A set of headlights bore down on them. "Someone's following us."

"You better hold on, then. I'm not going back."

She grabbed the handle above the door as he drove like a maniac around the corners and gunned it on the straightaways. When he got outside the city limits, he accelerated, and the next time she looked they were alone on the road. The darkness made it impossible to tell what kind of car had been tailing them. It could be the boss, or it could be someone else.

"Now, you'll tell me what's going on," Skylar demanded.

"It's a long story, and not very pretty. You sure?"

"Yes indeed," she said. "I'm a counselor, so nothing you can say will shock me."

He doubted that. God, he loved older women. They wore their femininity and sexuality like a charm bracelet, unashamed and confident. At least this one did.

Chapter 21

Vesta's eyes grew round and she clutched the door handle as Christopher Phillips rounded the last corner before the straightaway. He gripped the wheel tightly with one hand and threw his other arm out instinctively to hold her in her seat as he floored it, bouncing her around like a ping pong ball.

His wife and her friend were more trouble than they were worth, Vesta thought, though Christopher should blame no one but himself for that. Thank God she had tried to call him. He said he'd tried to both text and call Madison, and she hadn't answered for several hours after she said she'd be home. With a bad feeling about her safety, he drove to her house. She wasn't there. She hadn't said who she was going out with. Worried, he'd called Detective Little to report a possible crime.

He went home and stewed about it for an hour, then Vesta had called to see if he'd been the one to call it in. They met in the parking lot at the station. Feeling helpless and not knowing what else to do, Christopher checked the location app again. It showed Skylar in the condo, or at least her phone was there. But Vesta's gut feeling was that Madison, and maybe Skylar too, were in danger, despite the way Skylar had tried to reassure her on the phone.

They reached Skylar's condo and Christopher said, "There's activity in the alley." The detective's car was parked behind the complex. Vesta's misgivings about Detective Little were strong by this time and her anger at her partner went deep, especially after she had just begun to see them as romantic. Detective Little had not returned her repeated calls. Not only was the detective's car in the alley, someone else's was too. Now, coming out the back door was someone who looked like Skylar Phillips in nothing but a fishnet onesie, followed by a man.

Christopher gasped. He recognized her. His wife and some man climbed into a small, dark blue car and took off. Christopher's face transformed into a mask of fury. Not only was his blood boiling, his pride was taking a direct hit.

While they raced after the dark blue Corolla, she filled Christopher in on everything she knew about the case. It would break wide open now. She got on her phone and called for backup, but at this point it seemed up to her and Christopher to follow the Corolla and Skylar. The man in the car wasn't built like Tommy. Who was this guy, where was her the detective, and why hadn't Madison answered their calls?

Vesta called the state FBI contact and sent them to the condo. She also gave them a direction in which the vehicle they were chasing was headed. She and Christopher lost the car after the last curve. Now faced with three possible turns, they picked one, but they had chosen wrong. The road ended at an old cemetery. They backtracked and tried another road. Meanwhile, the probability that her Detective Little was the killer shook her to the core. It seemed ludicrous to think so.

***

Skylar undid her seatbelt as Nathaniel pulled his compact car up to the hut where he'd left Madison. She jumped out and rushed inside, oblivious to her unclothed state. Her friend was in severe pain, moaning softly. In spite of her condition, Madison managed to say, "My God, Skylar! Are you stripping now? Or just getting your kicks with anyone and everyone? What are you doing with Nathaniel?" She had some ripe things to say to him before Skylar could shush her.

"No more questions now. Please, Madison. We need to get you some help. You won't believe what's been happening."

Madison sniffed and her eyes grew rounder. "Have you been smoking weed?"

"Maybe...who wants to know?" Skylar said, winking.

"Well, put some clothes on, would you?"

Nathaniel returned carrying a picnic basket and a blanket. Both women looked at him like he was insane. He lifted the cooler and said, "Alcohol." He handed Skylar the blanket, which she wrapped around herself.

He cut the ropes holding Madison captive. "We've called the FBI and an ambulance, and they'll be here shortly, but you need to drink—a lot—to cut the pain. Let's look at your leg."

"Spoken like a true bartender," Skylar said. She and Nathaniel gently pulled Madison's pant leg up higher. When it wouldn't go, Nathaniel took out his knife and cut the cloth. The swelling around a huge bump had stretched the skin so tight it looked ready to burst open, and Skylar could well imagine how much agony Madison was experiencing. She'd need surgery.

"You got any hard liquor there?" Madison asked.

"Of course. A bartender is always well stocked. What's your preference? Scotch, rum, or vodka?"

"Mix 'em all, just hurry," she said.

He selected a bottle, and as he poured he said, "No, no, haven't you ever heard the saying, 'Beer before liquor, never been sicker. Liquor before beer, you're in the clear'? Actually, it's better to not mix them at all. Here, have some whiskey. Johnny Walker Green."

"Really? For me?"

He nodded and smiled, his cerulean blue eyes twinkling, seeming to forget for a moment what kind of trouble he was in, yet Skylar thought that after she got the whole story out of him in the car, he seemed oddly at peace.

"It'll hold you until someone gets here," Nathaniel said.

Madison upended the bottle and took a good long swig. Her eyes were glazed with pain.

"There's nowhere to sit in this joint," Skylar said.

Madison patted the mattress beside her, barely able to talk.

"No thanks."

"I know you're angry, Sky. I have things to be ashamed of. I hope to fix that when I get out of this mess." Silent tears rolled down her face. Pain or regret? Maybe both.

She sat on the mattress.

Nathaniel crouched across the room, only about ten feet away, hovering above the grimy floor.

"Don't worry, Nathaniel, you can probably get off on a plea bargain. You have plenty of info on your 'boss' that would be of value to law enforcement."

"I have done more damage than I can ever come to grips with," he said.

"It's going to take time to process things now that you've decided you can reject your former life for a new one. Be patient with yourself."

Nathaniel pointed to Madison, who had slumped over. "She's had enough to drink now," he said.

"No, look. She's only had a couple of ounces." Skylar held up the bottle to show him.

The flimsy wooden door burst open to admit Christopher and Vesta.

Skylar's eyes widened. "How'd you two get here?"

Vesta pointed to Madison. "What's wrong with her?"

"She just slumped over. We thought it was from the scotch, but we were just saying she's only had a couple of ounces. Her leg is broken."

Vesta glanced at the leg. "Oh my God." She placed two fingers on her neck. "Her heart's racing and she's breathing rapidly. I think she's thrown a blood clot to her lungs."

"We've got an ambulance coming," Nathaniel said.

Vesta lay Madison flat and looked at her leg. "This is bad." She gave Nathaniel a death look, and he took it.

Sirens wailed as they approached and then various uniforms filled the little hut, EMS evaluating and stabilizing Madison. "She's in cardiac arrest," a female voice shouted.

Chaos ensued while all nonessential persons cleared the hut.

Twenty minutes later one of the paramedics came out and shook his head. "I'm sorry. She didn't make it."

Skylar shrieked and pushed her way into the hut. The beautiful woman, her friend, lay peacefully, too peacefully, medical paraphernalia scattered around her from the valiant attempt made to save her life. Skylar pulled the blanket tighter around her and bent down, next to her only and best friend and partner in crime.

"I'm so sorry, Madison. I forgive you...I should have said it sooner." She wailed, rocking back and forth, everything else fading away and the impossibility of this reality shaking her to the core.

When she finally stood, a pair of big warm arms came around her, and in her grief they lent a degree of comfort, even though they came from her cheating husband.

"Come on, Skylar, they're waiting to take her. Everyone else has gone. I told them I'd stay with you and take you home."

"I don't know where home is, Christopher."

"I have an appointment this morning with the Bradshaws who I told you about yesterday. We have time to make it if you'd like to come."

"No, thank you, I can't. Let's go get some coffee. Things are so confusing right now, and I'm a mess. Maybe it would do us good to talk to each other for once. That hasn't happened in a long time."

He looked down, narrowing his eyes at her attire.

"It's not what it looks like," she said.

In spite of the terrible circumstances, he let his head fall back and he laughed. "And, it looks like Vesta's gonna need a new partner—again."

As they walked down the line of trees, lost in thought, a colorful swarm of migrating monarch butterflies detached from the branches in the early morning light and surrounded them in an orange and black cloud, their wings beating softly around the couple.

Maybe, just maybe, there was a chance for ex-lovers to have a new beginning.

Epilogue

The detective thought Briana would be the one to bring him peace the instant her lights went out. When that didn't do it, he figured he had one last chance. Skylar Phillips. The voices still visited him every night as they told him to keep killing. They said there were more women, and that all the unfaithful needed to go. His empty shot glass reminded him that the hardest part of the whole thing was seeing the women's eyes go dead. After the first two times, their empty eyes disturbed him so much that he had begun covering them before the final curtain went down.

Maybe next time would be the end of it, and he would at long last be free.

ABOUT THE AUTHOR

Lisa T. Horton is an author, life coach, and speaker. Lisa's passion for journaling and her love for mystery and adventure began with doing crossword puzzles. She believes the puzzles are like cases and the squares contain secrets.

Lisa was born and raised in Washington DC and has been married for over 20 years. She has four children and three grandchildren.

Through her writing and speaking, where she candidly shares her personal journey, Lisa focuses on helping women become all God created them to be.

She respectfully asks her readers for the courtesy of leaving her a review on Amazon.

www.ingramcontent.com/pod-product-compliance
Lightning Source LLC
Chambersburg PA
CBHW020611160726
47991CB00002BA/722